R. J. Parker's creative career began as a TV script writer, editor and producer. It was this background that fed into a series of cinematic, high-concept thrillers that grabs the reader from the very first page and doesn't release them until the last. R. J. Parker now lives in Salisbury.

THE
DINNER
PARTY

R. J. Parker

OneMoreChapter

One More Chapter
an imprint of HarperCollins*Publishers* Ltd
1 London Bridge Street
London SE1 9GF

www.harpercollins.co.uk

This paperback edition 2019
2

First published in Great Britain in ebook format
by HarperCollins*Publishers* 2019

A catalogue record for this book
is available from the British Library

ISBN: 978-0-00-835892-1

This novel is entirely a work of fiction.
The names, characters and incidents portrayed in it are
the work of the author's imagination. Any resemblance to
actual persons, living or dead, events or localities is
entirely coincidental.

Set in Birka by
Palimpsest Book Production Limited, Falkirk, Stirlingshire

Printed and bound in the UK

To Carole and Dave Whiteley, who know how to throw a dinner party.
Thanks for the support, guys!

Chapter 1

Ted awoke and felt like he'd been in a deep sleep. But as the bare leg he was clinging to slithered away from his sticky bloody fingers, the events that had left him sprawled on the kitchen floor crashed in. He'd blacked out for precious seconds and couldn't afford to again.

'Let go!' the owner of the leg spat.

He gripped the limb harder, dug his nails into their warm calf and skated forward on his front through the smeared blood on the granite tiles. If he relinquished the leg, he knew what would happen.

Their bodies thrashed around on the floor and noisily scattered metallic utensils. He tried to rise, but the object stuck in his back wouldn't allow him. It was a long stainless-steel prong, the type with a digital thermometer attached for testing the temperature of cooked meat. The acute pain along his spine severed his breath.

How deeply had it been planted in him? Was he paralyzed? He could still move his arms.

A scream.

It tugged his eyes open again. Consciousness was as slippery as his grasp on the leg, which jerked from under him as a bare foot caught him full in the face. The harsh impact deadened his hearing, warm blood filled his left nostril and darkness closed on his thoughts like a snare.

Wake up!

But his internal voice scarcely penetrated the barrier his brain was erecting against the assault.

Wake up.

No urgency in the muffled command now. He was withdrawing, leaving physical sensations far behind. Oblivion beckoned.

'Ted!'

His eyelids shot open. The return to the kitchen was as painful as the injuries to his body.

His hand was empty. They'd got free. The consequences of that rushed into him as fast as the room.

'Ted!'

Chapter 2

Three Days Earlier

'Ted!'

Ted was halfway up the stairs when the doorbell went.

'That'll be Evie and Jakob!' Juliette yelled from the bathroom.

The couple were always half an hour early. He and Juliette – after nightmare train journeys home – hadn't been in for longer than ten minutes. Ted descended the stairs and trotted up the hallway to the front door. Behind its frosted pane two figures stood in the dark. He switched on the outside light.

'Do you want us to drive around the block?' Evie apologized as soon as he opened up.

Ted could only see the middle of their faces in their scarves and hats. 'Come in before you freeze to the doorstep.' He gestured them in and lightly kissed Evie's cheek.

'The traffic was surprisingly clear for a Friday night,'

Jakob mitigated. He'd lived in the UK since his mid-teens, but his Norwegian accent had never been watered down. He rubbed his palms as he entered.

'I've just lit the wood burner.' Ted shook Jakob's freezing hand. 'You know where to hang your coats.' He made his way back to the candlelit kitchen dining room at the rear of the house. He'd been looking forward to tonight all week. And had taken the coming Monday to Wednesday of next week off work to redecorate. He loved his career as an independent assessor, but he was looking forward to having zero foster care compliance forms to process for a whole five days. 'Alexa, play my dinner party music.' He wondered if his guests would like his playlist. They all had strong opinions about music, so certain artists had to be avoided.

The device on the counter between the kitchen and the dining area glowed blue, but nothing happened. He could hear Evie remonstrating with Jakob that he'd made them leave too early. Jakob hated being late as much as he did though. He waited for them to hang their coats on the banister then led them into the dining area. 'We're doing Negronis for those who aren't driving.' He indicated the bottles assembled on the counter.

Evie's flushed complexion brightened. Even with her auburn curls in disarray after removing her claret beret, she looked really well. She'd been in remission for a good few months, but she and Jakob hadn't told anybody about their ordeal. They'd dropped off the social radar for a while, but everyone's lives were so busy it hadn't really registered. It was so good to see them both. 'I can't believe it was last May since we all got together.'

Evie nodded and focused on the bottles. 'Have you got Aperol instead of Campari? I'll be flat out after one otherwise.'

'Got some here somewhere.' Ted went to the cupboard the other side of the counter. 'Jakob?' He'd tried to call him Jake in the past but, after a few beers one night, Jakob had made it clear he didn't appreciate it.

'Nothing at the moment, I'll have some wine with my food.'

Which meant the usual. Jakob would abstain for half the evening, have a glass, quickly polish off a whole bottle and then call them a cab. Ted turned to him with a wry smile. 'Sure?'

'Positive.' Jakob nodded earnestly.

Not even a glimmer that Jakob knew exactly how the evening would unfold. Until he had that first glass, it would be strait-laced Jakob. After alcohol, the louder, red-faced and indiscreet version would appear. Ted was looking forward to him.

'What's bubbling in there?' Jakob eyed the slow cooker.

'Venison haunch in red wine, since this morning.'

Jakob nodded his approval and flattened the blonde wisps of hat hair that stuck out from the right side of his head. 'I'm starving.' His hand scrabbled in the bowl of peanuts on the counter.

'Warm yourselves up.' Ted nodded to the tubular burner in the old fireplace but noticed it had gone out.

'Don't worry. I'll see to that.' Jakob fisted some nuts into his mouth and went to stoke it.

Jakob had put on a few pounds since they'd last met. He was over six feet and thickset, but he had a definite paunch developing. All the couples coming were around the same age as he and Juliette. Ted had a good metabolism, but even running hadn't shifted his extra Christmas weight. Did he really have another five years grace until he was forty? His older work colleagues assured him that was when everything started to conform to gravity.

'Smells really good.' Evie tugged the sleeves of her black sweater over her pale hands, leaned on the counter and fixed him with her green eyes.

He was slightly relieved to have the counter between them and felt as he always did when it suddenly seemed like it was just the two of them. He'd never told Evie, but she reminded him of a ginger-haired classroom assistant he'd had a crush on at school. And she frequently made him feel like he was back in the playground. Particularly as, like Jakob, she was a teacher. 'Trip to the fjords still happening this year?' Ted knew it was an ongoing saga.

She pursed her lips. 'No. It's all about money and time ... and still money.'

Jakob hadn't been home to see his family for years. They were spread all over Norway and a trip had been on the cards since Ted could remember. He felt for Jakob but understood the limits of a teacher's salary.

'Do you have any more kindling?' Jakob turned from where he was crouching at the burner.

'Should be some in the bucket.'

Jakob shook his head at Ted and inverted the metal pail for good measure.

'Why haven't our guests got drinks in their hands?' Juliette was standing in the kitchen doorway.

It was miraculous. Only minutes ago, she'd got home from logging traffic pollution samples in Woolwich, windswept and exhausted, and now she was made up. Her silver-grey bob was immaculate, and she was wearing the olive-green woollen dress he'd bought her for her birthday. Juliette never took longer than ten minutes to get ready in the bathroom, but always looked like she'd spent hours there. Ted was glad to see her smile. Her father had passed away the previous September and she'd seemed very preoccupied over the last few weeks.

Evie embraced her, and Jakob quickly made his way over to give her a bear hug.

'It's been months since we've seen you.' Jakob crushed then released her. 'When was it?'

'Last May,' Evie reminded him.

Ted went to fix the cocktails. 'Alexa, play dinner party music.'

The device glowed blue again but still didn't obey.

Chapter 3

Ted used the downstairs bathroom, zipped himself up and checked his reflection in the mirror over the sink. Even in the bright light his complexion appeared pale and grubby, his blue eyes tired. He threw some water in his face and dried it with the hand towel, running his fingers through his straggly hazel hair and deciding it looked even worse. It didn't bother him that much, but he didn't want to let Juliette down. He headed back down the rear passage to the kitchen. Juliette was just opening a bag of ice. Orla and Connor had arrived. Now they were just waiting for the last two latecomers. 'Just going to check on Georgie.'

'He's not himself.' Juliette dropped some of the cubes into glasses.

'The usual?'

'I think so.'

Ted headed upstairs to Georgie's room. He'd only seen him briefly today as he'd been too busy getting things ready for the evening, but he always tucked him in. When he opened the bedroom door his six-year-old son was in his pyjamas, his fair hair dark and wet and combed straight. He sat cross-legged on top of his SpongeBob duvet, wearing headphones that were plugged into a tablet. Ted gestured for him to remove them and he did so. 'Hope we're not too noisy, scout.'

'No. I know you've all got to let off some steam.'

Ted smiled. Georgie had an unerring knack of absorbing adult phrases and using them in exactly the right context. 'Had a shower?' It was Georgie's new thing: he took a shower most nights and spent at least half an hour in there. Ted was concerned about the water consumption, but Juliette wanted to encourage his interest in hygiene. 'Everything OK at Peta's house today?' But Ted knew the childminder wasn't the problem.

'Fine.' Georgie wriggled on his behind uncomfortably.

Ted crossed the room and sat on the bed. 'What about at school?' Georgie breathed heavily through his nose and Ted could see his distress building. 'Is it Jolian again?'

Georgie swallowed hard and his ears twitched. They protruded and it made him an easy target for name-calling. 'Not just Jolian.'

'Who?'

'Tyrone, Yash ... Brendan.'

'I thought Brendan was your best buddy.'

Georgie nodded and narrowed his eyes at the screen. Ted could see how anxious he was. 'So has Jolian been getting them to gang up on you again?'

Georgie nodded.

'Then they're not worth your time.' What could he say when, as far as Georgie was concerned, his universe had ended? 'I know school's hard but, believe me, you'll find real friends soon. Proper ones. You thought these boys were but sometimes people aren't what they seem. Sometimes they have what we call ulterior motives.'

'What are they?' Georgie clearly liked the sound of the phrase.

'Stuff they want from you but don't tell you to your face.'

'Like my Xbox games?'

'That sort of thing. Point is, if your friends do exactly what Jolian says and turn on you, then they're really not worth knowing, are they?'

Georgie looked up at him, anguish in his eyes. 'But I've still got an invite to Brendan's party.'

'When is it?'

'March the sixth.'

'That's nearly two months away.' Two months was a long time in the social life of a child. 'You can decide whether you want to go then.'

Georgie straightened his back in mortification. 'But I *do* want to go.'

'But remember Brendan will want to come to yours the month after. That's when *you* decide whether he's been a good enough friend.' They'd had Brendan around a few times. He was spoilt, so Ted knew what was coming next.

'His party will be better than mine.'

'Why d'you say that?'

Georgie seemed to know why but clammed up.

Ted knew it was wrong, but he didn't like Brendan. Didn't like a six-year-old boy who still had to grow up. He was a bad influence on Georgie. Had already told him that Santa didn't exist. At six! 'We can do anything here you could do at Brendan's.'

'Yeah ... I know.'

But Georgie was sparing his feelings. Brendan's parents had a huge Georgian house with a games den. Georgie only had a playroom in the garage and that was damp and full of junk. It would be a big expense to make it properly habitable. 'Look, I've got to get back to the guests now, but we'll talk about this in the morning. OK?'

'There's nothing to talk about. I'll be OK. Really.'

Ted could feel his heart starting to break. 'It's Friday. Two whole days of no school. Try not to worry. If you show them that what they say doesn't bother you at all, they'll move on to somebody else. And if they don't, we'll both figure out a way of making them stop. Deal?'

'How about I take a kickboxing class?'

Ted smirked. 'I don't think we need to do anything that drastic. Come on, it's past lights out.'

'But I've only just started my screen time.'

'We'll roll it over to tomorrow.' Ted gestured for him to climb into bed and he scrambled under the duvet. 'We'll work it out.'

The doorbell rang.

'Who's that?'

'And don't play for time. Football training in the morning.' Ted kissed his hair and it smelt like he'd used too much shampoo. 'Don't worry about a thing, scout. It'll be a different story this time next week.' It probably would be, but he guessed that Jolian and Brendan were going to be the topic of many more conversations to come.

'Night, Dad.'

He'd only recently started taking the DY off Daddy and Ted wasn't sure he liked it. 'Sleep tight.' Ted got up, closed the door quietly and went downstairs. He met Juliette in the hallway. 'Half an hour's not too bad for the Driscolls.'

It was 'KathRhys' at the door. At least that was how they signed their greetings cards as a couple. The others all shared history, but Kathryn and Rhys had only moved to Basildon in 2017. Rhys worked for a petrochemical company that had relocated there and Kathryn was a recruitment consultant. Even though they lived the closest, only a five-minute drive away, they were always the last to arrive.

This rankled with Ted and more so with Jakob, even though Jakob had been instrumental in recruiting them to the dinner group. When they held up everyone else's evening, they never apologized for being late, so Ted had taken to inviting them an hour early to exert some damage limitation. 'Here they are!' he exclaimed, diplomatically, when he opened the door.

'Hope you haven't started without us.' Rhys's breath clouded around his dark bearded face. He was thirty-four, a year younger than Ted but his frameless spectacles gave him an avuncular appearance.

Tall Kathryn had her dark hair in a bun on top of her head and her usual dyed Mallen Streak forelock swept across the top of her fringe. She thrust a bag containing wine bottles into Ted's hands as if it was their 'Get Out of Jail Free' card and kissed him on the cheek.

'Some interesting ones in there.' Rhys nodded at the bag.

Ted didn't have a clue about wine, but he'd worked out that Rhys didn't either. Rhys was enthusiastic about whichever acidic consignment he'd been sent by his wine club, but Ted always put them on the rack to gather dust. At their next visit Rhys would forget that he'd brought them previously and examine the labels with vague disdain. Ted didn't dislike Kathryn and Rhys. They just weren't his favourite people. They didn't really fit in with the rest of the group, but they were Evie and Jakob's friends and had assumed one invite to join them all for dinner in 2017 meant lifelong membership.

But when Juliette's father died, Kathryn and Rhys had been incredibly supportive. Both spending time with her because they'd both lived through the same bereavement. More time than any of their other friends. After that Ted's perception had changed. They were at odds with the others, but Ted couldn't forget the sensitive side they'd shown his wife when she'd really needed it.

'The girls are sleeping over at a friend's, but they didn't want us to leave,' Kathryn said to Juliette.

Kathryn and Rhys had twins of Georgie's age. It had taken them five years of IVF treatment to bring them into the world, so Ted understood why they handled their girls like antique china.

He took Kathryn's dark teal cashmere shawl and it smelt overpoweringly of perfume. 'Come through.' That was everybody. The evening was now officially underway.

Chapter 4

'It's a trust game.' Evie gauged seven people's reactions and didn't seem surprised by them: attentiveness from the women and uncomfortable suspicion from the men.

'Alexa, turn off,' Juliette said without shifting her attention from Evie.

Ed Sheeran was cut off mid-angst. That pleased Ted, but he was still baffled as to why Alexa only seemed to obey Juliette. The sudden silence committed everyone to listen and he studied Orla's and Connor's expressions. Evie attempting to reconcile them was part of every get-together.

Orla and Connor were a passive aggressive couple, their Northern Irish accents noticeably stronger when they were tossing cutting remarks at each other. But now they sat among the others like two singletons. Juliette liked to mix everyone up so nobody was sitting with their partner. They'd never been that tactile but now the only giveaway that they were actually together was the occasional barked remonstration from Orla when Connor rested his elbows on the table or slouched in his chair.

Connor's look was always the same – wiry, sweaty and harried, with three buttons opened down from the collar, his tight black curls looking as coiled as he was. But today Ted could see a shadow of something in Connor's eyes. Orla was as skinny and tall as Connor and her straight fringe of mousy hair came exactly down to her eyebrow line. She was a pale and beautiful woman, but Ted thought the style made her look slightly deranged. Juliette had told him her eyebrows had fallen out because of a childhood trauma and that she'd always been self-conscious about them. She'd never wanted to augment them with eyeliner or get them tattooed, however, even though a large percentage of her arms were covered in ink. Ted thought she looked more frazzled than usual.

'My work colleague is seeing a counsellor at the moment,' Evie continued. 'She said that after twelve years of marriage she didn't believe anyone outside of it was ever going to be able to help her.'

There was that 'work colleague' again. Ted wondered if she really existed. Evie was always advocating therapy, even though she and Jakob had had only a handful of sessions some years ago. They were a solid couple, but boredom was their enemy. Evie often looked for problems where there weren't any. They should have had children; it had been talked about at one point, but Juliette said the subject was now strictly out of bounds.

'He got them to play the trust game. It's especially for couples who have been married longer than seven years.'

That described all of them. Kathryn and Rhys had had their tenth anniversary already and, as they'd all got married the same year, the rest of them would be celebrating this coming summer.

Orla and Connor had two girls, like Kathryn and Rhys. Ted didn't know how they managed with more than one child. But they'd all felt overpowered by parenthood at various stages, experienced that deep fatigue and the night terrors about their children's future. Probably because of the girls, Evie had made Orla and Connor her rescue project, and recently even Ted had become concerned about Connor.

Connor had always had a dour sense of humour, but over the past year there had been a marked change in his personality. The flippant glimmer in his eye had gone and he now seemed to go through social occasions with Orla on autopilot. But it was something Connor had said at a pub that had disturbed Ted. Connor had been bemoaning the relentless nature of parental commitments and Ted had responded with a platitude about trying to enjoy the kids when they were young because life was short. Connor had said:

'Life's short. But sometimes not short enough.'

It was vintage Connor, but without a trace of his usual playfulness. He just looked worn out. He was an investment broker and brought home a bigger salary than the other couples put together, but Ted guessed that juggling multiple stress balls at work and dealing with a crumbling marriage was the reason he was becoming increasingly withdrawn. Maybe Ted had been reading too much about suicide stats for men their age, but he'd been worried enough to mention it to Juliette. She said that Orla and Connor's fights had stopped, but that seemed more troubling than anything else.

'To any couple who feel they've amassed too much baggage, the game is designed to expunge guilt and wipe the slate clean for the sake of their futures.'

Ted's eyes switched to Evie and back to Connor again. His friend's face was impassive.

'So what is the game?' Juliette asked as she poured more red wine from the decanter into the empty glasses on the table.

Jakob nodded he'd have more. He'd just finished his third glass and his ruddy complexion held the tally. He'd already told Evie they'd be getting a cab.

'Each person in a couple has to write down their deepest, darkest secret on a piece of paper, something that has happened since they took their vows – something they've never told their partner about.' Evie checked their reactions again, gave it a beat to let the tension set in.

Nobody moved. Ted had been about to swallow but now didn't want to fill the silence.

'Then they fold the piece of paper, put it into an envelope and give it to their partner.'

'Uh-huh.' Jakob responded offhandedly and took a generous swig of his filled glass. 'Already sounds dangerous.'

Evie turned to him. 'If you have something to hide.'

'What if they have nothing to hide?' Rhys absently stroked his beard.

Evie ignored him. 'It can be anything, minor or major. Then their partner, without opening the envelope, tells them that they forgive them and sets fire to it.'

'What about the other's envelope?' Juliette filled her own glass.

'They do the same. Say they forgive them and burn theirs too.'

Juliette's eyes were fixed on pouring.

'And what the hell does that achieve?' Connor sounded bored.

'It's symbolic and it means they can move on. Whatever secret they had has been forgiven and destroyed by their partner.'

'Without them knowing what it was,' said Rhys warily.

'It's a declaration of faith in each other's future together.' Evie sipped her wine.

Connor leaned back in his chair. 'Isn't that like ten Hail Marys though? I mean, how often do you do this? Every week? Do I simply get Orla to absolve me every time I do something wrong?'

'That's already a full-time job.' Orla didn't look at him when she said it, just gently stroked the ornate tattoo of a blue-ringed octopus on her forearm.

'Why do you assume you're the only one who's done wrong?' Juliette asked Connor pointedly.

The three men were briefly tongue-tied.

'It's not like a laundry service.' Evie fingered the stem of her glass. 'You're not taking this seriously.'

Was Juliette? Ted noticed she still hadn't made eye contact with him.

'And it's one secret you write down?' Rhys raised an eyebrow.

Evie sighed. 'Yes.'

'So nobody could do a job lot and get them all forgiven and burnt in one hit?' Rhys glanced at Kathryn.

'So what happened to just being honest and open with your wife?' Connor seemed to regret the question before he'd finished asking it.

'What indeed.' Orla's Northern Irish accent was suddenly very thick.

Jakob was shaking his head at his wine glass.

'You've gone very quiet, darling,' Evie observed.

'Let people sort their own problems out,' Jakob said quietly and took another glug of wine. 'No need to spoil a nice evening.'

Evie frowned theatrically. 'I'm just telling them about my work colleague.'

Jakob kept his nose in the glass, his eyes rolling.

'I'd be happy to do it,' Orla declared. She nodded as attention shifted to her. 'Why not?'

Ted felt the atmosphere suddenly chill. 'Nobody here is a qualified therapist.' He shot a glance to Evie then Juliette, but both were looking at Orla. It felt like the evening was suddenly on shaky ground.

'I'll do it too,' Kathryn proclaimed.

'So you've already thought of something to write down?' Rhys wasn't smiling.

'OK. Why don't I get some pens and paper?' Juliette was on her feet.

'Wait.'

She fixed Ted blankly and it reminded him of how she looked at Georgie with dead-eyed patience when he threw a tantrum.

'Not everyone's comfortable with this.'

Juliette looked around the table and Ted followed suit. The other women were obviously keen on the idea. Connor leant back in his chair and languidly raised his hands.

'Looks like we've been set up,' he said with resignation. 'We're damned if we do, but we're most certainly damned if we don't.'

Jakob put down his empty glass. 'Get the paper, if Evie wants to forgive me so badly.'

'For what?' Evie tried to read his features.

'You'll never know. Your game, remember?'

Ted knew that strait-laced Jakob wouldn't have played.

'OK then?' Juliette smiled at Ted, as if to reassure him that the game wasn't for them. But when she turned away, Ted saw it quickly vanish.

Chapter 5

'You didn't have to think long either,' Kathryn remarked icily and flattened her Mallen Streak to her forehead.

Rhys had his fingers cupped around the piece of paper he was scribbling on, his tongue protruding through his beard in concentration. 'Ouch.' He shook his aching hand. 'Can't remember the last time I had to write anything more than my signature.' But still he hadn't finished.

'You're going to run out of space in a minute.' A sly smile tugged at the corner of Connor's mouth.

Nobody else was joining in. Ted regarded the blank pastel notepaper and empty envelopes that Juliette had placed in front of everyone.

'Well … I'm not doing this on my own.' Rhys looked around guardedly at the others.

Nobody put a hand to the pile of pens in the middle of the table. Jakob had his arms folded defensively.

Connor turned to Evie. 'And this worked for your colleague?'

Evie nodded.

'How?' Ted asked.

'Well, she's no longer divorcing her husband.' Evie pursed her lips.

'Maybe you can invite her along to our next evening so we can compare notes,' Connor retorted dryly.

'Yes, it would be good to meet her at last.' Jakob straightened in his seat but didn't uncross his arms. 'What about you, Evie? You started this.' He raised one fair eyebrow at her.

Evie put down her wine glass.

'Well, I suppose as *my* husband is so eager.' Kathryn eyed the pens.

'It's my suggestion. Jakob's right.' Evie plucked a pen and started to write on her paper.

'No thinking time for you either?' Jakob emptied the remains of the decanter into his glass.

Evie ignored him, finished and folded her piece of paper in half.

'I'll get us some more wine.' Juliette scraped her chair out.

'Is that a good idea?' Ted had already counted four bottles opened between them. Another one wasn't exactly going to improve the atmosphere.

'Don't look so worried.' Juliette began to rise.

'Hang on.' Rhys held out his hand to her. 'You don't get out of it that easily.' He folded his piece of paper. 'I'm done. I'll get the wine.' He slid it inside its powder blue envelope and fixed his gaze on Evie. 'Do we seal them?'

'I suppose so.' She slipped hers into her peach envelope. Juliette settled back in her chair.

'OK.' Rhys made a show of licking the edge obscenely while he looked at Kathryn. Then he placed it delicately on the table and thumped it a couple of times with his fist.

As if in retaliation, Kathryn reached past him and snatched up a pen.

'Shall I select something from the rack?' Rhys headed to where it was mounted on the wall.

'Whatever you fancy.' Ted was watching the glances Orla was throwing Connor.

'Crack on then.' Orla nodded at the pens.

'Then we can change the subject and have some cheese and port?' Connor seized one.

'Yes.' Orla followed suit. 'God forbid we should talk about anything meaningful.' Her hand moved across the paper.

Ted suspected it was too late to prevent what Evie had instigated but tried regardless. 'Maybe we should do this another time. It *is* getting late.'

Juliette picked up a pen. 'Come on. We don't want to be the last.'

'Very suspicious,' Rhys chuckled. 'I wonder what a therapist would read into that?'

When Juliette started writing, Ted began to feel uneasy. Jakob caught his eye. 'What if we can't think of anything?'

Evie bit her lip. 'You'll think of something.'

Jakob shook his head. 'So, there's obviously something *you* think I should write.'

'Whatever you feel guilty about. Could be a small thing, could be a very big thing.' She let that hang between them for a few seconds. 'You'll think of something.' Evie nodded at the pens.

Jakob sighed, reluctantly grabbed one and started scratching at his paper.

'We've got to have a talk about your wine cellar.' Rhys peered at the bottle he'd withdrawn from the bottom of the rack.

Ted knew it was a Rhys leftover. 'Better ones at the top.'

Rhys squinted at them through his specs. 'If you say so.'

But suddenly Ted realized he was the only person who hadn't written anything. He looked at the top of Juliette's silver-grey bob as she concentrated. What could he commit to paper? Not *that*. He couldn't put that moment into words, couldn't physically register what he didn't even want to think about. Not for the sake of Evie's stupid party game.

But Juliette had to forgive him for whatever was in the envelope, burn it to release him from guilt. Was he tempted enough to risk giving the secret a physical presence before it was willingly destroyed? No. Think of something else. This was just a silly stunt. He'd drunk too much wine. If they were all sober, they'd all recognize how foolish this was.

Juliette's pen moved across the paper. What exactly was she writing?

Chapter 6

'I forgive you, Rhys.' Kathryn was holding Rhys's powder blue envelope in her hand. In the other she had a green transparent plastic lighter that Juliette had found.

'That was pretty convincing.' Rhys smiled humourlessly.

'We all have to say it with conviction. Right, Evie?' Kathryn's eyes remained on Rhys.

Ted registered that Evie seemed transfixed by the couple facing each other over the table.

Kathryn rasped the flint of the lighter with her thumb and a flame flickered up towards the bottom edge of the envelope. She moved it closer and positioned both over the handcrafted yellow clay ashtray from Portugal that Ted's parents had brought back for them.

Kathryn touched the flame to the paper, and it started to blacken, but after a few seconds, she extinguished the lighter and bit her lip. 'I could just open it. What if I do that?'

Evie fingered an auburn lock behind her ear. 'It's not allowed. The trust has been placed in your hands.'

Kathryn seemed to enjoy Rhys's uncomfortable expression. 'Might be worth it.'

'Are you forgetting that Rhys has your envelope?' Jakob slurred.

'Perhaps I don't mind him seeing what's in mine. Maybe opening them would be more honest than burning them.'

'Maybe you're right. Your choice, pumpkin.' Rhys sucked on the hairs under his lip.

Now Ted wanted his own envelope back, wished he'd listened to his common sense. But the idea of having Juliette forgive him for what he'd written had been too difficult to resist.

Kathryn lowered the lighter. 'Maybe there's nothing but rubbish on mine.' She was clearly relishing the moment.

'Then you've cheated.' Connor didn't sound amused. 'And if that's the case, nobody plays.'

Orla eyed his lemon envelope. 'Eager for me to burn yours then? We could all just open them now.'

But Evie interjected. 'Stop teasing, Kathryn. Or hand him back the envelope. The sole purpose of the game is to release the past and unite for the sake of the future.'

'You seem very keen to do that, Evie.' Jakob reached for his glass, but it was empty.

Kathryn smiled at Rhys, then flicked the flint again. She played the lighter over the bottom of the envelope and the flames licked up the paper. She released it when they reached her French polished nails.

The envelope and its secret curled into black in the

ashtray and nobody spoke until the last patch of blue paper had vanished.

'I'd better open a window before we set the alarm off.' Ted was glad of the distraction, slid the pane behind him open and let the freezing air pour in. But nobody sitting around the table complained about the cold.

'My turn now.' Rhys held his hand out for the lighter.

'You can breathe,' Kathryn said caustically and passed it to him. She shoved the ashtray and it slid across the table.

Ted wondered exactly what she'd just forgiven Rhys for. And did she now feel foolish because she had?

Evie sat straight. 'We need a change in attitude here. This is to help us, not drive us apart. We're all willingly doing this.'

'Are we?' Ted countered.

Juliette turned slowly to him, playfulness gone and suspicion creeping into her expression. 'Yes. Or are you afraid I might open yours?' Her eyes flicked to his sealed orange envelope on the table in front of her.

'I just don't think this is going to lead anywhere good.' Ted shook his head too many times.

Juliette frowned at him, genuinely worried now.

'Let's just get this finished,' Connor said in a surly tone. 'Perhaps Evie will stop trying to analyse Orla and me then.'

'What's that supposed to mean?' Evie almost sounded mortified.

'Oh, come on.' Connor shook his head.

'Rhys, are you doing this?' Kathryn nodded at her husband; her expression was flushed.

'What's the matter, pumpkin? Feeling uncomfortable?' He grinned.

'Don't call me that.' Kathryn clenched her jaw.

Ted knew the menopause had arrived early for Kathryn. She was having what she described as one of her 'tropical moments' but she'd made it clear she didn't want people to fuss when it happened. Besides, the window was already open.

'Just get it done,' Jakob huffed.

Rhys nodded, held the lighter to the side of Kathryn's aquamarine envelope and paused for dramatic effect. 'I forgive you.'

'You have to mean it, Rhys,' Evie reminded him. 'Say it like you do.'

'OK.' Rhys nodded and some of the cruelty drained from his face. He wet his mouth. 'I forgive you.' His eyes still fixed on his wife, Rhys set fire to the envelope and let it drop into the ashtray.

Chapter 7

Jakob indicated the mint green envelope that contained his secret. 'Maybe you should have gone first, Evie.'

'Perhaps.' Evie held it up and studied the seal.

Ted watched Jakob examine his empty glass and then the unopened bottle that Rhys had selected at the opposite end of the table. Looked like the game was sobering everybody up. It had definitely caused a fractious atmosphere between each couple, including him and Juliette. He just wanted it over now. He suspected he'd be calling cabs soon.

'Show us how it's done then.' Jakob interlinked his fingers on the table and sat forward.

Rhys slid the smoking ashtray and the lighter down the table to where they were sitting. Jakob took them, positioned the ashtray in front of Evie and handed her the lighter.

She took it and maintained eye contact with him. 'I forgive you.' She smiled earnestly and blinked, then set fire to the green envelope.

But Ted noticed the side of her mouth twitch as the paper was consumed.

'Don't get your fingers burned.' Jakob nodded at the envelope.

But Evie held it for a while longer before letting what little remained float down into the ashtray.

'That's you off the hook, Jakob,' Orla said flatly. 'Put the girl out of her misery.'

'Or just open it and find out how imperfect everyone is,' Connor added.

'Connor,' Orla growled.

'I forgot, Evie's rules.' Connor emphasized her name.

It struck Ted how painfully aware Orla and Connor were of Evie's attempts to mend their relationship and just how offended they might be.

Jakob picked up Evie's peach envelope from the table and turned it over in his hands.

Evie tightened her bottom lip at him, and Ted could see the nervousness in her green eyes. He suddenly felt sorry for her. She *had* brought the evening down, *had* made everyone feel uncomfortable, but her heart was in the right place. She wanted Orla and Connor to be happy again, for their sake and their children's, but this was the ultimate example of her misguided attempts causing more harm than good.

Evie went to pass the lighter to Jakob, but he took a butter knife off the table instead.

'Jakob.' When Juliette spoke there was more than a warning in her tone. 'Don't.'

31

Ted knew Jakob would listen to Juliette. He always respected her opinion.

'This is what happens when you play with fire, Evie. Let's hope that's the one take-home you get from this.'

Ted didn't like the spite in Jakob's comment.

Jakob put the blade of the knife to the flap of the sealed peach envelope and then grinned at Evie. 'I forgive you,' he said melodramatically. He put the knife down, took the lighter from her and set fire to the envelope.

Evie's face didn't shift, but Ted could see her shoulders slightly drop.

'Shit.' Jakob released the flaming envelope as it reached his fingers.

The paper seemed to burn more intensely than the others and then went out.

'Looks like Evie's secret is the hottest,' Rhys quipped.

Orla didn't even allow the awkward laughter to subside. 'Us now then.' She impatiently extended her hand and Jakob passed the ashtray and lighter. She held Connor's lemon envelope rigidly between her thumb and forefinger and immediately flicked the flint. It sparked but didn't work.

'Looks like Connor's is fireproof.'

Everyone ignored Rhys.

She hastily spun the flint with her thumb several more times before it lit. Connor's envelope started to smoke.

'You've got to say it,' Kathryn reminded her.

She robotically cocked her face to Connor. 'I forgive you.'

'Me too.' Connor leaned across and held Orla's coral envelope in the same flame.

The guests watched their envelopes feed off each other's heat. Connor discarded his and then Orla released hers.

'There. Satisfied?' But Orla didn't look at Evie.

Connor broke the silence. 'Well, it made a nice change from Orla getting me to swear faithfulness to her on my mother's life. Cheese and port now?'

Ted gently shook his head. It had seriously misfired. The only people that hadn't been fazed by Evie's game were the couple she wanted to fix. It was everyone else who had been tested by it. But his orange envelope still lay in front of Juliette. 'Let's get ours out of the way then.' He reached over and took the ashtray. Orla gave him the lighter. He slid both to Juliette.

She looked up at him with a tiny frown.

Had he seemed too eager? There was a long silence and then Rhys smiled smugly at him. 'In a bit of a hurry, Ted?' He twisted off the lid of the wine bottle.

Ted nodded at Juliette's lavender envelope in front of him. 'I'll do yours first, if you like.' He attempted to sound casual instead of defensive but failed. 'Let's just get this finished.'

'OK.' But Juliette sounded far from it.

Everyone's eyes were on him. 'And I don't think we should drink anything more, Rhys,' he deflected. 'Evie's game hasn't exactly put everyone in the best frame of mind.' Ted picked up Juliette's lavender envelope and studiously examined it. 'Mine or yours then?'

'I'd better do yours,' Juliette stated coolly and seized the lighter.

'Dad!' Georgie shouted from upstairs.

From the tone in his voice, it didn't sound like an emergency. Ted waited and Juliette raised her eyebrows.

'Dad!'

'You'd better go.' She hadn't lit the envelope.

As he lingered he looked at everyone's perplexed expressions.

'Dad!'

'Perfect timing.' He tried to sound jovial. 'Back now.' Ted rose and made for the hallway door.

'Wait,' Juliette said.

He turned and her eyes fell on the lavender envelope in his hand. It contained her secret. Had she thought he might read it in private? He set it on the table and walked leisurely from the room, resisting the temptation to tell them not to do anything without him.

Only as he mounted the stairs did he hear the buzz of conversation begin again.

Chapter 8

'You smell funny, Dad,' Georgie said after he'd been tucked back in.

Ted had just kissed the side of his head. 'It's just grown-up drinks.'

'Are your teeth black again?' Georgie kept his eyes closed.

'Probably.' Ted wondered what was going on downstairs. 'What time is it?'

'Way past sleep time.' Ted squinted at his watch. It was gone midnight. 'We'll be coming to bed soon.'

'After you've finished playing your games?'

Ted paused. 'Have you been listening?' He knew Georgie frequently came halfway down the stairs to eavesdrop on the adults.

'No. You're just very loud. You woke me up.'

Ted was sure they hadn't been making that much noise. The music was off, and Evie's game had seen to the rest. 'OK, we'll try to be quieter. No more getting up though.'

'Promise.' Georgie shut his eyes tighter.

Ted paused at the door. 'You're not still worrying about your friends?'

'No. Not thinking about them.'

But Ted guessed Georgie was telling him what he wanted to hear.

'It's wine o'clock.' Georgie must have heard Juliette say that multiple times. 'Go, Dad.'

'OK, sleep tight.' Ted pulled the door shut behind him, wondering if he should have stayed to talk. But this wasn't the right time and he'd already said they'd discuss it in the morning.

As he made his way back down the stairs he could hear Rhys's raucous laugh. Hopefully, that was a good sign. He tried to enter the dining room as calmly as possible, but the chatter instantly died down.

Juliette turned from the table as he approached, maternal concern overriding everything else. 'Is he OK?'

'Fine. Thought we were being a bit loud.'

Rhys exaggeratedly clapped his hand over his mouth.

Ted walked to his place at the table and sat. Filled his glass, took a sip and gazed around as if he'd forgotten exactly what they were in the middle of. He didn't look directly at his envelope but could see the orange blur in front of Juliette.

'I didn't think you wanted anything else to drink.' Juliette's face resumed its earlier suspicion.

'As everyone else has had a refill ...' He nodded at the others' glasses. 'Right. Us then,' Ted sighed, as if it were a chore. Now he regarded the thankfully sealed envelope in front of Juliette.

Juliette took hold of the lighter and flicked up a flame. She didn't touch the envelope though. 'Sure you want me to do this?' She held the glow at face height so that her blue eyes were either side of it.

Ted shrugged. 'You didn't steam it open while I was with Georgie?' Rhys said something in response, but Ted didn't hear it.

Juliette's face remained unchanged, her pupils locked on his and suddenly they were the only two people in the room.

'OK.' Juliette eventually glanced down at the orange envelope, picked it up and held the lighter to it. 'I forgive you.' But she only looked at the paper as it went up.

Ted wondered how he should react. He was aware of himself slowly nodding, of his stomach muscles relaxing.

Juliette kept her eyes on the envelope as it shrivelled in the ashtray. She scrutinized its blackened form for a moment, as if waiting for something to happen, and then blew the ash into fragments. 'There, gone.'

Tiny pieces briefly hovered above the table before coming to rest there.

Ted didn't wait for her eyes to return to his. 'OK, just yours left.' He wouldn't milk the moment as some of the others had.

She put the lighter on the side of the ashtray, gently pushed it over to him and sat back.

Ted took her lavender envelope in one hand and the lighter in the other, holding both over the ashtray. When he refocused on Juliette, however, he found an emotion on her face he hadn't expected. He'd been anticipating disapproval, a portent of a heated conversation to come, but Ted saw something he rarely did. Juliette looked scared. It unnerved him.

'I forgive you.' Ted quickly lit the envelope, as if doing so would also incinerate the fear in her expression. The flames burned between them. He dropped it and as the veil of smoke cleared her countenance changed. She was taking in the other guests now, smiling for their benefit.

'Any other games?' Jakob ribbed Evie.

She shook her head, stony-faced.

Rhys chuckled. The atmosphere of the room washed back in, as if all the tension had been blown away, and Ted suddenly felt a chill from the open window behind him.

The guests started chatting again, all except Ted and Juliette.

'OK, cheese and port *now*?' Connor asked impatiently.

Juliette nodded and started to rise.

'I'll get it.' Ted stood faster. 'I'll shut this window now we're done.' He turned to the pane and sealed it against the darkness outside.

Strained conversation continued as he unwrapped the cheese behind the counter. He contemplated the ashtray on the table and wondered what unspoken moments hidden within four marriages had just been cremated. And even though they'd now been willingly reduced to ash, he was sure Evie's game had given them more of a presence than they'd had before the eight of them had agreed to play.

Chapter 9

Conversation was perfunctory as Ted and Juliette tidied after their guests had left. Even when most of the dishes were in the washer, the group's unease still hung about the dining room. They decided to finish clearing up the following day. Juliette blew out the candles and they headed for the bedroom.

Ted listened at Georgie's door to the sound of his heavy breathing. He nodded to Juliette that all was fine, and they padded into their room.

'Have you made this year's payment for the green collection bin yet?' Juliette asked, as they both brushed their teeth, naked, in the en suite.

Ted sighed. He'd meant to do that a handful of times. 'Sorry, remind me first thing.'

Juliette nodded but said nothing else, her toothbrush angled right to the back of her mouth and toothpaste foam running over her knuckles.

Ted was desperate to discuss Evie's game. Wanted to reassure Juliette that the sudden apprehension between them was misplaced. He wished he'd put his foot down when Evie had suggested it. But Juliette had been more than OK about participating. Was that because she had nothing whatsoever to hide? But she *had* written something down. Was it significant or had she just scribbled something minor for the sake of joining in? And why had she looked so scared? They'd both forgiven each other, but now they would think of nothing else until they'd talked about it.

Even though he needed to, he knew this wasn't the time. Besides, if he broached the subject he'd look even guiltier. He'd been too eager for her to burn his envelope and the whole table had noticed. He should have bided his time like Juliette.

She had a cooler head than him, could keep a secret when it mattered. She'd sprung surprise parties on him for his birthday and, when he'd thought back to the lies she'd calmly told to conceal them, he'd wondered if she'd ever used the same subterfuge to hide anything else. He was a hopeless liar. And maybe that was why she was acting like she was now.

Or was that to deflect her guilt? It seemed inconceivable that she'd been unfaithful to him. Did she still harbour doubts about his fidelity? She'd given him a hard time when they'd first started going out, got quite paranoid that he was seeing someone else. It had seemed like a huge compliment. He'd been so amazed that Juliette had even been interested in him at the time, so the idea she thought he was *that* in demand was a considerable boost to his self-esteem. That was when she'd tested him and sent him a valentine card from a girl she'd invented, to see if he would tell her about it. He did. He passed.

He considered what he would say if she asked him directly about what had been in his envelope. He would tell the truth, but that sounded easier in his head than in reality. Maybe they'd never have the conversation because neither of them wanted to divulge what they'd written. The best thing to do was wipe the slate clean and move on.

Juliette spat her toothpaste out, gargled and spat again and walked into the bedroom without meeting his eye.

How long would he have to ride this one out? Till tomorrow, for a few days or whenever the argument broke? He finished at the sink and switched off the light.

The lamp was on at Juliette's side of the bed, but she'd clicked it off before he got in. That didn't bode well. Juliette always snuggled down and read her Kindle, only her hands protruding from the duvet, and usually only turned off the lamp when the screen had fallen against her nose. But suddenly her warm hands held his face.

'I love you,' her minty lips kissed him in the darkness. Then she released him.

'Love you too.' But he sensed she didn't want him to try to find her mouth again.

Juliette turned her back to him, as if she wanted him to nuzzle her shoulders. He did and her body nestled into him.

Ted felt relief but was sure her eyes remained open as well. He was still checking the time at three o'clock and knew Juliette was too. But not long after 3.40 her breathing became shallow and Ted fell asleep.

At 4.02 they were both wrenched awake. After a moment, Ted realized it was the sound of their landline ringing. It very rarely rang now, and Juliette had suggested they disconnect it as most people used their personal numbers. Ted scrabbled for it on his side of the bed.

'Quick, before it wakes Georgie.' Juliette sounded groggy.

Ted knocked a framed photo of him and Juliette off the bedside, as he frantically searched for the handset. Sounded like the glass had broken. He squinted at the phone's glowing green keys and tried to remember which one was answer. It had already rung a good few times. He focused and punched the pick-up button. 'Hello?'

The line was dead.

'They hung up,' he explained.

They both hated getting phone calls in the middle of the night. The last one had been about Juliette's father. Ted heard her swallow.

Then a muted buzzing started.

'That's mine.' Juliette sat up.

'Where is it?'

Juliette turned on her lamp, scrabbled naked out of bed and grabbed her phone from her handbag on a dressing table chair under the curtained window. 'One missed call. Hello?'

Ted hinged upright, his circulation thudding between his eyes.

'Evie?' Juliette frowned. The only sound was muffled shouting on the other end of the line. 'Wait, slow down.'

Evie. Why the hell was she calling at this hour?

'Evie, take a breath.'

Even from the bed, Ted could hear Evie's voice yelling in Juliette's ear. What was going on?

'OK, OK. Tell him I'm coming. I'll talk to him about it. We're on our way. Evie?' Juliette glanced at the screen. 'She hung up.' Juliette speed-dialled her number. 'It's gone to message.'

'What's happening?'

Juliette shook her head and tried again.

Chapter 10

'Any update?' Ted emerged from the bathroom wearing the taupe shirt and black jeans he'd had on earlier.

'She's still not picking up.' Juliette had put on grey slacks and a navy sweatshirt.

'Let me try Jakob.' Ted speed-dialled with his phone but got his message. 'No luck. So what exactly did she say?'

'Just that Jakob had gone berserk. I couldn't understand anymore.'

'Should we call the police?'

'She called *us*. If we were having a fight, would you want the police turning up?'

'So they're definitely having a fight?'

'From what I could understand.'

'I'd better get round there.' Ted scanned the bright room for his shoes.

'I'm going too. Evie's my friend.' She slipped on some black suede ankle boots.

'We can't leave Georgie on his own.'

'I've spoken to Zoe. She's on her way round.'

Ted shook his head. 'You shouldn't have disturbed her at this hour.'

'She was up with Pip anyway.'

Their next-door neighbour had an eight-month-old daughter, so she and Juliette often babysat for each other. 'That's a big ask.'

'I'm sure I'll return the favour.'

Ted slid his feet into his leather shoes. 'All right, I'll get the car.'

'You can't drive. You were still drinking a couple of hours ago. I've ordered a cab and it's nearly here.'

'That was fast work.' As he'd thrown water in his face to wake himself and then dressed he thought Juliette had been talking to Evie.

Juliette picked her phone up from the bed and checked the cab's progress. 'Let's be ready to go as soon as it arrives.' She tucked the phone in her back pocket and headed for the door.

Ted followed and they both paused at Georgie's. No sound from within.

'We won't wake him,' Juliette whispered. 'Zoe can let him know what's happening when he does.'

Ted kept his voice low too. 'Hopefully, we'll be back before he's up.'

Juliette said nothing and stepped carefully down the stairs.

As they reached the bottom somebody knocked lightly on the front door. Juliette crept up the hallway runner and opened it. 'Hi Zoe, you should have used your key.'

'I didn't like to when you were in.' She whispered too. Zoe Cabot was a young single mother, in her mid-twenties. She was gently bouncing her new baby. She wore a paisley headscarf and a worried expression. Her pale eyelashes rapidly blinked. 'Everything OK?'

Juliette nodded. 'Just a little emergency, friends of ours in Ibbotson. I'll phone you when we know what's going on. Help yourself to anything you want. Georgie is usually up at seven on Saturday.'

Zoe nodded gravely at Juliette and then put on a warm smile for Ted. 'Don't worry about anything here.' She dumped down a changing bag.

A car beeped.

'Really appreciate you doing this.' Ted stood aside so she could squeeze by, grabbed his leather coat from the rack and hurried out into the dark. There was a frost on their small front lawn, and he zipped up and shivered as he trotted to the car outside the gate. Juliette remained inside, so he greeted the driver of the white Seat, sat in the front and pulled his door shut.

'Ibbotson, please. Just waiting for my wife.'

The young Japanese driver nodded and there was a short awkward delay until Juliette dropped into the back seat.

'Zoe all right?'

Juliette closed her door and didn't answer Ted immediately. 'She's fine.'

'You OK?'

Again her response was delayed. 'Yes, just worried about Evie.'

The driver pulled out.

'They're only fifteen minutes away. We'll soon find out what's going on.' But Ted suspected it was serious. Evie had never called them like this before. It was difficult to imagine them even raising their voices to each other. Who knew what went on behind closed doors though? Jakob *had* been very quiet when they left and pretty unsteady on his feet. 'Try her again.'

Juliette did, then shook her head and hung up.

The driver turned left at the end of the street.

'What was Jakob doing?'

'I told you I don't know.'

'So what's "it"?'

Juliette leaned forward and replied in the ear furthest from the driver. 'What d'you mean?'

Ted turned. 'When you were on the phone to Evie you said you'd talk to him about "it". What is "it"?'

'She just said he'd gone berserk. The rest was incoherent.'

'There's nothing you're not telling me?'

'Why would there be?'

Ted wondered if there was a little too much mortification in her response. 'You just seem so determined to come with me.'

'I told you, she's my friend.'

'Has this happened before. Them fighting?'

'I don't think so.'

Ted turned front again. He couldn't imagine it. There was sometimes sniping between them, but Jakob always seemed to be a gentle giant.

They drove the rest of the way to Ibbotson in silence.

Chapter 11

The small hamlet that Evie and Jakob lived in had very few streetlights and the narrow road that ran through it was often manned by retired residents taking speeding drivers' registration numbers. Ted had been caught on more than one occasion and had received stiff letters through the post. He wouldn't have been surprised to find pensioners with clipboards lurking in the hedges even at this hour of the morning.

The driver took the sharp right into Fencham Place and the headlights illuminated a tall hedge that bordered the left side. Evie and Jakob's redbrick Victorian house was opposite the crossroads at the end. Lights burned in the downstairs and upstairs windows.

'This is it. Just drop us in front of here,' Juliette instructed.

The driver did and she paid him.

'D'you mind waiting?' Ted asked.

'It's OK.' Juliette gave him a tip. 'We might be a while.'

As soon as they got out, he pulled away without a word.

They both crunched up the long, gravelled driveway. Ted studied the lit panes for either of their friends, but there was no movement.

He rang the bell. No sound of anyone coming to answer it. Ted tried again and Juliette thumped the panel with her fist. He stood back from the door and scanned the windows above.

'Evie!' Juliette yelled and banged a second time.

'Call her again. I'll try Jakob.'

She did but shook her head.

He left a message. 'Jakob, let us in. We're outside your front door and we're worried about Evie. Please ring me straight away.' He hung up. 'They don't have a landline?'

'No. Let's try the back.'

Ted felt uneasy as he followed Juliette down the side of the house to the rear of the property. Maybe they were upstairs having a tête-à-tête, but surely they would have heard them at the door. Something felt badly wrong.

The glass door to the kitchen was wide open. The light was on, the room empty.

Ted peered at the darkened lawn. 'Anybody out here?' he said loudly. His breath drifted back to him, but the only response was the muted sound of the motorway.

Juliette had already stepped over the threshold and edged across the wooden tiled floor to the breakfast bar in the middle of the kitchen. The polished tiles were Jakob's pride and joy. He'd rescued them from a gutted church nearby and lovingly laid them there, all the way through the hall and into the dining room.

'Evie? Jakob? We're coming in!' There was a nervous tremor in Juliette's voice. She reached the sealed door into the hallway and paused. 'I'll try her again.' She hit Evie's number.

A loud extract of Funktown America's 'Celebrate Good Times' made them both jump and their attention shifted to the phone vibrating on the floor in the kitchen.

Ted walked over to where it lay beneath the sink unit, then froze.

'What is it?' Juliette joined him there and examined it more closely too.

There were dark smears over the handset.

'That *is* blood, isn't it?' Ted straightened.

Juliette nodded and turned back to the sealed door. 'Wait. We should be careful.'

There was panic in Juliette's eyes. 'Call the police?'

'Yes.' Ted took out his phone.

A series of thumps from above them. They both looked upwards. Sounded like somebody walking across the floor.

Juliette hurried to the door, but Ted intercepted her there. 'I'll shout up the stairs. If there's any sign of trouble we should both leave.'

Juliette nodded.

Before Ted could open the door they heard more thumping. 'They're coming down the stairs.' He swung it wide and they hastened along a darkened passage with three open doors off it that led to the hallway. They glanced into each deserted room they passed. The third was the familiar dining area where they'd spent many an evening, the chairs tucked neatly under the long table at its centre.

When they reached the hallway, they heard the front door click shut. The light was on, but nobody was at the bottom of the stairs.

'Have they just left?' Juliette rushed to the front door and opened it.

They could hear the sound of receding footsteps on gravel.

'Evie! Jakob!' Juliette shouted.

They both held their breath and under the sound of his thudding circulation Ted heard the footsteps falter and stop.

'It's Juliette!'

They both gazed into the pitch blackness.

Then the footsteps started again and picked up speed.

Chapter 12

'Maybe that wasn't Evie or Jakob,' Ted said as soon as the footfalls had faded.

Juliette turned to Ted in alarm and then directed her attention back to the hallway.

Ted closed the door.

'Evie!' Juliette called up the stairs. 'Jakob!'

No response.

Ted clenched his stomach, put his palm on the banister and took the first couple of steps slowly, their boards creaking under the dark-blue carpet. His mouth was already dry.

Juliette was right behind him. 'Be careful,' she whispered.

She was right. There could still be intruders in the house. Maybe Evie and Jakob were lying injured upstairs. His pace quickened. But they were there because of an argument between the couple. Could there really be anyone else involved?

They reached the landing and found five closed doors.

'Evie?' Juliette's voice sounded loud in the enclosed space.

Ted had never been upstairs in their house. There was a

downstairs bathroom, which they used when they visited, so he'd never had any reason to.

'Jakob?' Juliette said quieter.

'Look.' Ted pointed.

There was a long smudge of blood at shoulder height along the right-hand wall.

They both halted.

'Ring the police.' Ted whispered and didn't take his eyes from the stain. All he could hear was their breathing.

Juliette took out her phone and dialled. 'Police,' she hissed.

While she relayed the specifics, Ted seized the nearest door handle.

Juliette put her hand firmly on his. 'OK. As fast as you can though.' She hung up. 'They said we should leave the house immediately and wait for them outside.'

'But they could be hurt.'

'They're sending an ambulance.'

'God knows how quickly that will arrive though.' Ted kept his grip on the door. 'Somebody fled. I'm not leaving if either of them could be bleeding up here and need our help.'

'Nobody's answered us.'

'They could be unconscious.'

She bit her lip.

He could tell how shaken she was by what they'd found but already knew what her reaction would be to what he suggested next. 'Go and wait outside while I look.'

Juliette shook her head resolutely. 'We do it now, quickly.'

'Sure?' But Ted knew it was pointless arguing.

'Evie?' She called again.

They both listened to the silence for a moment.

Both their breathing stopped as he depressed the handle, the spring in the mechanism creaking as he pushed inside.

The large sparsely decorated space looked like an office, with only a table and swivel chair skulking under the window. The blinds were sealed. An open laptop glowed on the desk and illuminated the empty room. There was nobody here.

They moved down the passage and Juliette opened the next right-hand door.

It was a spotless bathroom: nobody inside and no signs of a disturbance. The heat from the towel radiators and an aroma of tea tree oil rolled out at them.

Ted was at the third left door first. These had to be the bedrooms. 'Jakob.' But he didn't wait for an answer.

It was a spare room. A double bed made up, but lots of paperwork and magazines stacked on the duvet.

Juliette had already moved to the last two doors at the end of the passage. 'Evie?'

Ted opened the one nearest to him. It probably used to be a bedroom but now it was a generous changing room with doorless wardrobes along the right wall. Evie's clothes took up considerably more space than Jakob's. He recognized the outfit Evie had been wearing lying on top of a laundry basket. A familiar feminine scent hung around the room. No trace of a struggle in here either.

There was only one door left to open and they both paused outside. This had to be the main bedroom.

Ted yanked the handle down but stayed where he was as the panel swung wide. It bumped against the wall as they took in its interior.

No Evie or Jakob and the king-size was still made.

Juliette switched on the light and the bulb buzzed overhead.

'So the argument started before they went to bed.'

'Look.' Juliette nodded to the far side of the room.

There was brown blood smeared on the long radiator under the window.

She crossed to examine it and Ted joined her there. On the oatmeal carpet in front of it were more dark red patches. The heat from the radiator had dried the fingerprint stains but the ones on the floor still looked wet.

Ted scanned the rest of the carpet. 'Let's not touch anything.'

'We'd better go outside.' Juliette gulped. 'I don't want to be in here.'

Ted was about to move when the light in the room changed. He turned to the window and realized the security light had come on at the rear. A cat was slinking across the back lawn. 'Motion detector.'

But Juliette moved her face closer to the pane. 'Is that ...?'

Ted followed her gaze. Somebody was lying on the frosted grass by the summerhouse.

Chapter 13

Ted and Juliette raced back down the stairs, across the hallway, along the passage and through the kitchen to the lawn. Just as they reached it the security light went out shrouding them in darkness again.

Ted waved his arms and it lit up once more. The person lying on their back by the summerhouse was about thirty yards away and as his feet crunched over the crisp grass he could see dark footprints leading to them.

'Evie!' Juliette bolted past him when she recognized who it was.

Ted was close behind and knelt with her beside Evie. Their friend was barefoot and wearing only a magenta silk night robe, which had ridden up her waist. There was a dark patch of blood around the right side of her head and red marks on her throat.

'Evie.' Juliette put a shaking hand to her face. 'She's cold.'

Ted gripped Evie's icy bare shoulder. As he did a tiny wisp of breath escaped her lips. 'Evie.'

She didn't stir.

'Evie.' He shook her.

Juliette put a finger behind Evie's ear. 'I can't feel a pulse. Wake up!'

Ted tried mouth-to-mouth. Her lips were freezing. He'd forgotten his training but was sure chest compressions were more important. Interlinking his fingers he started pumping the lower half of her sternum.

'Evie, stay with us!' Juliette slapped her face.

He kept going, tried breathing into her mouth again. She tasted of alcohol. 'Evie!'

He could hear Juliette on the phone yelling for an ambulance as he frantically shifted position and put his weight behind his wrists. Wasn't there a danger of breaking ribs? He kept going.

Her eyes half opened.

'Evie?' Ted shifted back so his shadow wasn't obscuring her face.

But there was nothing in her pupils.

'Evie!' Juliette held her hand tightly.

No more vapour from her mouth.

'She was just breathing.' Juliette jerked her arm.

But Ted assumed it had been trapped air. She was dead.

Juliette continued to shake her and Ted, dazed, surveyed the shadowy hedges. Could whoever have done this be watching them? But they'd heard someone sprint down the driveway and, as he was nowhere inside the house, it was very likely to have been Jakob. What the hell had happened? 'Juliette ...'

She was still clutching Evie's wrist.

Both his hands were trembling. 'I don't think we should touch her anymore.'

'This is ...' Words failed her, and her eyes bulged with tears.

'We should go to the front of the house. I'll let the police know what's happened.'

Juliette looked at him as if he were insane. 'I'm not leaving her.'

'I understand ...' His breath caught in his chest. He was as shell-shocked as she was. He wanted to embrace her so that she didn't have to look at Evie's body. But her features were set. 'But this is a crime scene now ...' Ted examined their footprints intermingled with the others.

'We're in it already. I'm not moving.' Her attention shifted back to Evie and a tear dropped from one eye onto her lap. 'Where the hell does he think he can run to?'

Ted was thinking the same. Jakob had clearly gone mad. He knew alcohol changed his personality, but he'd never seen him get aggressive with Evie. They were such a stable couple. That's what was so horrifying. And recently Evie's cancer treatment had seemed to cement their relationship. He recalled how Jakob had told him how it made him re-evaluate everything afterwards. That nothing he stressed about before seemed significant in the face of losing his wife.

Juliette shook her head. 'If we could have got here sooner ... Minutes sooner.'

'We got here as quickly as we could.' But Evie had still been alive forty minutes before. If they'd told the cab driver to put his foot down, would they have arrived in time?

Juliette unstuck a red curl that was plastered to Evie's face.

'Juliette, you mustn't.' Only hours before Ted had kissed Evie's cheek.

Juliette retracted her hand.

The security light went out and Ted got to his feet to wave his arms at the house. The lawn was bathed once more. His legs quaked.

Juliette pulled Evie's robe down.

'Juliette,' he cautioned.

She ignored him and tugged it over Evie's exposed thighs.

Ted knew there was no doubt what had done this. It was Evie's game. That's what had altered the entire evening. Jakob had seemed fine when they arrived.

Was this how paper-thin the wall was between the happiness Evie and Jakob appeared to have and what had just happened? Ted had seen how the notion of unspoken secrets had instantly engendered hostility between their friends. Had one or both of them revealed what had been written on their piece of paper?

Juliette closed her eyes. 'Maybe I didn't know them at all.'

Ted briefly wondered what might have transpired if he and Juliette had revealed each other's secrets while they'd been lying awake in bed.

Juliette abruptly opened her eyes again.

They could hear a vehicle rolling up the gravel at the front of the house.

Chapter 14

'I'll stay with her.' Juliette nodded for Ted to go.

Ted opened his mouth and then closed it again. He briefly squeezed her shoulder, turned and shakily headed back down the lawn. The lights of the car illuminated the side of the house and he shielded his eyes as he approached the vehicle.

A man got out of the passenger's side. 'Sir?'

The light went out as the engine was switched off, but Ted could see it was a police car. 'It's OK, I ... my wife called you.'

Another man emerged from the driver's side.

'We've just found our friend. She's been ... she's been killed.' The words sounded absurd.

The two officers exchanged a glance.

'Where is she?' The passenger asked uneasily.

Ted wondered if either of them was equipped to deal with a situation like this. They probably thought they were being called out to a routine domestic. 'She's on the back lawn.'

Momentarily, neither of the officers seemed to know what to do.

'I'll take you there.' Ted started to turn.

'Wait.' The driver closed his door. 'Who are you?'

'Ted Middleton. My wife and I are friends of Evie and Jakob ... Eriksson. Evie called us and said she and her husband were having an argument. We got a cab out here. When we arrived somebody ran from the house. We think it was Jakob.'

'Her husband?'

'Yes,' Ted confirmed to the driver.

'You're not sure?' He seemed suspicious.

Even though it had only happened minutes ago, Ted struggled to get his thoughts in order. 'Nobody answered, so we went in through the open back door. Someone ran down the stairs and then left via the drive. And Jakob's not in the house.'

'Let the station know,' the driver said to his passenger. 'I'll take a look.'

'Shouldn't we just wait for a senior officer?' The passenger's voice quivered.

Ted wondered how old they were. 'My wife is with the body. I don't want to leave her there any longer.'

'Call the station. I'll secure the scene.' The driver tried to imbue his voice with confidence. 'Lead the way.'

Ted nodded and turned. They reached the lawn just as the light went out again. He waved his hands and the scene was floodlit. Glancing sideways he confirmed that the uniformed officer was barely in his twenties. His head was closely shaved, and his lean features were grimacing in readiness for what was to come. Ted led him to where Juliette was still crouching and heard him inhale sharply through his nose as they crunched across the grass.

'I'm Constable Adams,' he said to Juliette.

Juliette exchanged a look with Ted.

'There are other officers on the way,' Adams reassured her and fell silent as he stared at Evie. 'You're sure she's dead?'

Juliette nodded and wiped an eye with her thumb.

'If I can just ask you both to step out.' Adams offered her his hand to get up.

Juliette didn't take it and stood. 'What happens now?'

'If you don't mind waiting with my colleague in the meantime, I can handle things here.' But he didn't sound convinced.

'I'd rather not leave her.'

Adams hesitated. 'No, wait in the car and keep warm. Someone will take statements from you shortly.'

Juliette looked down at Evie.

'Come on.' Ted put his hand gently under her left arm, but she didn't budge.

'She needs to be covered,' she told the officer.

He nodded. 'That'll be done. I do have to ask you to vacate the scene now though.'

Juliette started to take off her jacket.

'Juliette ...' Ted gripped her arm tighter.

'Please, madam. You'll be making the job for forensics even harder.'

Juliette paused and then nodded.

'Come on. Let him do his job.' Ted tried to lead her gently away, but still she stood rooted to the spot.

The three of them regarded Evie's body for a few moments and then Juliette walked unsteadily back down the lawn.

'She'll be OK.'

Ted didn't answer the officer.

Chapter 15

Both still anaesthetized by their experience, Ted and Juliette waited in the dark street in the back of the patrol car. It smelt of Olbas Oil. Ted took out his phone and tapped Jakob's number. Would he have his with him? He dialled and waited. Perhaps it was ringing in the house.

'Who are you calling? Zoe?'

'No, Jakob.'

'Hang up,' Juliette said sharply. 'The police have to deal with him now.'

She was right. But he waited for another ring.

'Ted!'

He hung up. 'I can't get my head around this.'

'You'll have to tell the officer what you did.'

He nodded distractedly as Juliette rang Zoe and told her they were talking to the police and would explain everything at home.

They waited for twenty minutes, observing various vehicles drawing up, until an unmarked car parked directly behind them. Ted turned as a squat man in a heavy dark-woollen overcoat and black hunting hat with flaps covering his ears emerged and noisily trudged down the gravel drive to the rear of the house.

Quarter of an hour later, he returned and approached the patrol car. He opened the back passenger door. 'Mr and Mrs Middleton?'

Ted got out and took in the man's wide and pockmarked features. There was a wisp of a dark moustache clinging to the top of his lip that seemed to be covering a cleft palate scar.

'I'm Detective Inspector Renton. Are you keeping warm enough in there?' He clumped his hands together, which were clad in leather gloves.

'We're fine.' Ted folded his arms against the cold.

Juliette closed her door and joined them on the pavement. 'Our son is with a neighbour, so we'd like to get back to him as soon as we can.'

'Of course.' Renton blew out a cloud of breath.

Ted got a whiff of curry. 'We've already given a statement to one officer.'

Renton sniffed. 'So you knew the deceased well?'

They both nodded.

'I'll need you to be more specific. Old friends?'

'Yes,' Ted replied first.

Renton shifted his dark eyes to Juliette. 'Very close friends?'

'I've known Evie since high school.' Juliette shivered and pulled her collar closer to her neck.

'Have they had physical fights like this before?'

'No,' she retorted categorically.

'At least, not that we know of.' Ted noticed Juliette glance at him.

Renton darted his pupils between them and settled on Ted. 'And her husband. You knew him well?'

'Yes. They were at our house this evening. For dinner,' Ted added.

'And how were they acting towards each other then?'

'A little drunk. That's all,' Juliette answered him.

Renton didn't shift his eyes from Ted. 'You'd all been drinking?'

'Red wine mostly.' Even though he'd brushed his teeth Ted could still taste it.

'But no big fallouts?'

'No.' Ted felt that was the truth.

'What time did they leave?'

'About one.' Ted cleared his throat. Why did he feel so nervous?

'And as far as you were concerned, there was no hostility between them?'

'Until Evie called us,' Juliette responded quickly.

Ted had been about to tell the DI about the game they'd played.

Renton fixed Juliette. 'So who picked up the phone to her?'

'I did.' She rubbed the edges of her arms through her jacket. 'She was screaming that Jakob had gone berserk.'

'So you rushed over here in a cab?'

'She was hysterical. We tried her again, didn't we?'

Ted nodded.

Juliette continued. 'But she didn't pick up. When we got here we called her from the doorstep, Jakob as well. But there was still no answer.'

'So you got in through the back. Without any trouble?'

'We know the house. We've been here on lots of occasions.' Juliette turned to Ted again. 'Haven't we?'

But Ted was feeling uneasy. There had been an exchange between Juliette and Evie on the phone. And was she deliberately not mentioning Evie's game?

'Where have you come from?' Renton shifted his gaze back to Ted.

'Just on the edge of Basildon. The Russell estate.' He was sure Renton had picked up on Juliette monopolizing their account.

'You both saw her husband leaving the property?'

Ted spoke before Juliette could. 'We only assumed it was him. We'd come in from the back and heard a noise upstairs. By the time we reached the hallway he'd left through the front.'

'He?'

Ted pursed his lips. 'Well, we couldn't actually see them. Just heard them running over the gravel.'

'So it might have been someone else?'

'Yes,' Juliette sighed. 'But Jakob's not here, so it's likely—'

'Let's just stick with the facts. You didn't see a man?'

'No,' Ted confirmed. 'Just heard someone.'

'Then you went upstairs?'

Ted looked to the house. 'Yes. Opened the doors and found the rooms empty. Then we spotted Evie on the lawn.'

'And she was dead when you reached her?'

'Yes,' Juliette said, pointedly.

Renton slapped his hands together again.

Ted knew he had to confess. 'I'm sorry, while we were waiting here I tried calling Jakob.'

'That was ... ill-advised,' Renton exhaled.

'I'm sorry.'

'His phone's in the house though. He left without it. Apart from the obvious was there any other reason you needed to talk to him?'

'No. I'm sorry.' Ted felt foolish.

'What time was that?'

'About half an hour ago.'

'You'll have to leave your number.'

'No problem.'

'So, it was just the four of you tonight?'

Ted didn't wait for Juliette. 'Eight of us.'

'OK.' Renton blinked thoughtfully. 'I'd like you to give me the names and contact details of the others.'

Chapter 16

Juliette called them a taxi and the skies were still dark when it dropped them outside their front gate. Neither of them had said anything during the journey. Ted considered that Juliette might be in a deeper state of shock than she appeared. But he had to ask the question and after their cab pulled away he put a hand gently on her shoulder. She was just about to put her key in the front door.

'Why didn't you tell Renton about the game?'

She turned to him, puffy fatigue in her eyes. 'What would have been the point?'

'He asked if there was any hostility between them here.'

'But there wasn't.' She frowned.

'Don't say you didn't notice how Jakob's mood changed.'

'He always gets that way after a few glasses of wine.'

That was true.

'And they seemed fine when they left. Just drunk.' She slid her key in the lock.

'I don't know. Jakob was very quiet.'

Juliette didn't enter the house.

'And you can't deny that it caused an atmosphere between the two of us. Maybe it started an argument when they got home.'

'I suppose.' She turned again, blinking, as if it had only just occurred to her.

It couldn't have. She seemed eager to avoid telling Renton about the dinner party. 'Are you worried the police will think we were all to blame for starting their argument?'

'Just ... don't say that.' Juliette bit back emotion.

Ted didn't want to upset her anymore than she was. 'It was Evie's idea. She wanted to play it. Not everyone wanted to.'

She sniffed. 'Including you.'

'I could see where it was going.'

Juliette regarded him with mortification. 'To Jakob murdering Evie?'

'Of course not. If that *is* what happened.'

Juliette shook her head. 'Evie's dead. Jakob attacked her and ran off. Where the hell does he think he can hide?'

'We didn't see him.'

'Are you really defending him?'

'No. We just don't know exactly what happened. What did she say to you?'

'On the phone?'

'Yes.'

'That he'd gone berserk. She was distraught.'

Ted was sure Juliette was still withholding something. 'That was all?'

72

Juliette's gaze hardened. 'I was half-awake.'

'If you're worried that you agreed to play that trust game ...'

She briefly closed her eyes. 'I'm not. We all did. It was just that ... a game.'

'If Renton talks to the others they're going to tell him about it.'

'Then OK. If he talks to them ...'

'He's bound to. I just think we should have been the first.'

'I think he was more concerned about the alcohol that was consumed.'

'We all drank a little too much.' Ted knew they shouldn't be arguing like this. Juliette had lost her best friend. He took a breath and lowered his voice. 'Keep remembering, the trust game was Evie's idea. Just because it happened around our table ...'

'Let's forget it.' She swallowed hard. 'Maybe Renton is going to be suspicious because *you* tried to call Jakob.'

'I know that was stupid, but anybody could do it. I'm sure Jakob will hand himself in, if he hasn't already. Then we'll know exactly what happened.'

'Will we? We'll have his account. We'll never hear Evie's side.'

They both fell silent as they allowed that to sink in.

Ted knew neither of them had even begun to absorb what had happened yet. It was all so surreal. Where was Jakob?

Juliette opened up and they found Zoe just inside the door bouncing Pip. She acted startled.

'You OK?' Ted stepped inside after Juliette.

'Sorry. I thought I heard a car dropping you off, but then you didn't come in.'

Ted wondered if she'd just listened to their entire conversation.

'What's happened? Why have you been talking to the police?' she asked anxiously.

Juliette inhaled. 'My friend Evie has been murdered.'

Zoe's mouth fell open.

As Juliette explained, Ted asked himself why he would feel so uncomfortable if Zoe *had* eavesdropped on their conversation. After all, they had nothing to hide.

Chapter 17

Ted checked on Georgie and he was still fast asleep, completely oblivious to their absence and what they'd just seen. His son's chest gently rose and fell, his face untroubled. He envied him.

Juliette had told him to rest, even if he couldn't sleep, and stayed downstairs with Zoe. They'd agreed to carry on the weekend as normal for Georgie's sake, and he would be up early for football practice at eight.

But when Ted entered their bedroom he knew he couldn't lie down or close his eyes. In the sudden silence he realized just how fast his heart was still beating. He picked up the photo frame that he'd knocked over and carefully put the glass shards into the bin.

He moved some clothes off one of the club chairs and sat down, body rigid. Glancing at his watch he could see it was nearly six. He could just hear Juliette talking low to Zoe in the dining room. Only hours ago Evie had been seated there and now she was probably getting zipped up in a bag. What the hell had happened between her leaving with Jakob and the crime scene on the lawn?

No matter how he'd tried to comfort Juliette, Ted knew the game was very likely the catalyst. Maybe she hadn't picked up on it, but Ted had registered how withdrawn Jakob had been when they left. Had he and Evie argued in their cab? That was definitely worth mentioning to Renton. Ted had called Greenaway Cabs, their trusted firm, so it wouldn't be difficult to track down their driver. It was usually one of three guys who came out to their address.

But maybe it had all blown up when they got home. Did Jakob need to know his wife's secret, or had it been the other way round? He considered whether he should call Kathryn, Rhys, Orla and Connor. They were all probably still sleeping. The detective hadn't forbidden Ted from contacting them, but he didn't want to ring anyone he shouldn't again.

He took the card that Renton had given him out of his back pocket. He'd said to get in touch with any other details and that he'd be speaking to them later that day. Were he and Juliette actually suspects? But their story would check out. There would be a record of the call to them early that morning, plus their driver would confirm he'd picked them up and dropped them off there. But there must have been ten minutes between them arriving and calling the police. And with Jakob missing they had been the only ones on the property when the patrol car had arrived. If Renton suspected them, however, surely he wouldn't have let them go.

But another thought occurred to him. Had their cab driver paid attention to any of the conversation they'd had on the way to Evie and Jakob's, when he'd questioned Juliette about withholding the specifics of her phone conversation with Evie? And they hadn't mentioned Evie's trust game to Renton. The others were bound to if they were questioned. How would that make them look?

Ted took a breath and told himself to stop panicking. They hadn't done anything wrong except respond to a friend in need. But Juliette's glossing over of what had happened at the dinner party still unsettled him. Was it because she just felt guilty?

Ted took his phone out. He would call Renton, tell him about the cab firm that picked up Evie and Jakob. Then he'd mention the trust game and that he thought Jakob had gone quiet afterwards and that Juliette hadn't registered it. Would talking about it now seem suspect? But it *was* just a stupid game. Better Renton had all the details before he spoke to the others. Ted squinted at the number on his card.

Call it.

The handset buzzed against his palm. Unknown caller. Renton? But it wasn't the number on the card. 'Hello?' There was a pause and Ted anticipated a recorded message telling him he'd won a prize.

'Ted?'

He immediately recognized the whispering voice. 'Jakob?'

'Who are you with?'

'I'm alone. Where are you?'

'Where are *you*?'

'We've just got back from your house. We found Evie …' How the hell could he broach the question he needed to ask? 'We … called the police.' He wanted to scream at him.

'I know what you're thinking. I didn't kill her, Ted.'

'What the hell happened?'

'You're sure you're alone? Where's Juliette?'

'Downstairs. You've got to give yourself up.'

'I want this conversation to remain between the two of us. No police.'

'Why?'

'Just say it will or I'm hanging up now.' Jakob's normally composed voice rose an octave.

'OK. Just stay on the line.'

Jakob sniffed harshly. 'I need to talk to you.'

'You need to talk to the police. How d'you think this looks?'

'I will do. But I need to speak to you first. Face to face.'

'Why?'

'I can't talk here. I'm on a public payphone.'

'Give yourself up. You shouldn't have run. The longer you leave it the guiltier you seem.'

'When can you get away?'

'I have to take Georgie to Roath Park at eight but—'

'On your own?'

78

'Yes. But I'm not—'

'I'll see you behind the pavilion on the other side of the park at ten past eight.'

'Jakob—'

'You promise you won't bring anyone else? No police.'

'Jakob.'

'Promise.'

Ted looked up and caught his reflection in the dressing table mirror, his expression as suspended as the moment.

'I'm hanging up then.'

'Wait. OK. I'll see you there. OK?'

'Behind the pavilion. You've promised this will stay between us. If there's anyone else with you, you won't see me.' Jakob cut the call.

Chapter 18

Ted remained seated, turning the phone over in his sweaty palms, and then noticed he could no longer hear voices downstairs. He rose and was about to open the door when Juliette did, apprehension on her face.

'You OK?' She frowned uneasily.

He nodded. Should he tell her about the conversation he'd just had? Jakob had made him promise though.

'Sure?'

He nodded again. He had to tell her, had to tell the police. He couldn't withhold anything else. But why had Jakob wanted to keep it between them? Could it explain the exchange Juliette had had with Evie on the phone before they'd gone to the house?

Juliette wiped a tear from her eye. 'Georgie's still sleeping.' She softly closed the door. 'How are we going to tell him?'

Ted sighed. He hadn't even considered that. 'And should we call the others?'

'I've just spoken to Kathryn.'

Ted was slightly taken aback. 'When?'

'After Zoe left.'

'Shouldn't we have asked Renton first?'

Juliette shrugged. 'Surely he would have told us if we couldn't.'

'But he said he wants to speak to them.'

'He took their details. Doesn't mean he's going to. And I'd rather the news came from me.' She sniffed and then opened her arms.

Ted embraced her. Her body was so cold. He hugged her tighter. It felt good.

'I can't believe it,' her lips said against his shoulder.

He shook his head. It would take them some time to process their ordeal. But if he was going to tell Juliette about the phone call from Jakob, now was the moment.

'Jakob must have lost his mind.'

And that's what Ted found the most difficult to accept. But he'd only seen him at their social gatherings, had no idea what went on between him and his wife at home. He tried to tell Juliette but again something stopped him. It felt like a whole minute passed. 'How was Kathryn?'

'I woke her up. She's in bits.'

'What about Orla and Connor?'

'I tried them too. Didn't get an answer.'

That was weird. It was only after six on a Saturday morning. But Ted knew that Orla had insomnia and often needed strong pills to sleep.

Juliette seemed to read his thoughts. 'They're probably out for the count.'

But Connor was one of those rare people who never got hangovers. 'You tried their landline?' Ted didn't want to let her go, didn't want to look into her eyes while he was harbouring a secret.

'Tried all their numbers. Left Orla a message to call me as soon as she got it.'

'I was about to call Renton.' He felt her tense.

'What for?'

Her mouth felt hot against his shirt. 'I thought we could give him the number of the cab firm that picked up Evie and Jakob.'

Her body remained rigid. 'Yes. We could do that,' she said listlessly.

She had to be running on empty. 'Maybe the driver can shed some light on what happened.'

'Good thinking,' she responded flatly. 'But you know what Jakob's like. He hates airing dirty washing in public. It probably all exploded when they got back.'

'And I thought we should mention the game.' He held his breath as he waited for her reaction.

She didn't stiffen anymore, just slightly nodded her head. 'Let's see what comes to light when they find Jakob. He's the only one who knows exactly what happened.'

Tell her. Tell her.

Juliette released Ted, rubbed her eyes and focused on the carpet. 'The fact he ran isn't a good sign though, is it?'

Something in that moment changed Ted's mind. He understood that Juliette was angry, bereaved and angry, but they still didn't know why Jakob ran. If that had been him they'd heard fleeing the house.

It was less than two hours until football practice. He could meet Jakob, find out what he had to say. Then persuade him to hand himself in and tell Juliette. If he didn't keep it a secret, he might not have the opportunity to talk Jakob round. Juliette would probably urge him to involve the police. And he wanted to hear from Jakob exactly how Evie ended up dead on the lawn. He couldn't accept the fact that he was capable of that.

Juliette looked up at him and her lips were tight. 'We'll know where he is soon.'

Chapter 19

'You're quiet back there.' Ted glanced in the mirror at his son strapped into his seat. They were on their way to Roath Park, but it had taken some time for him to notice Georgie's silence.

He didn't shift his attention from the side window.

'Still thinking about Jolian and Brendan?' That conversation seemed like a lifetime ago.

'No.'

Ted knew when he was fibbing.

'Are *you* OK, Dad?' Georgie stared through the pane.

'Don't change the subject. I don't want those boys to spoil your weekend. If there's problems next week, we'll sort them out together.'

'You didn't speak to me at breakfast time.'

'I'm sorry. Just a few things on my mind.' So it wasn't diversion tactics. Georgie had picked up on Ted's anxiety. He and Juliette had decided they would wait to hear from Renton before sitting their son down. Only when they had a full picture of what had happened could they even begin to work out how to tell him.

'Anything you want to talk about?'

Ted smiled. Georgie was replicating what he often said. 'No. I'm looking forward to seeing you in action though.'

Georgie met his eye in the mirror, but his smile was false. He knew he'd been fobbed off.

'You brought your tracksuit bottoms?'

Georgie shook his head.

'You're going to be freezing in just your shorts.' There was still frost on the grass verges either side of the car. Ted considered turning around and returning home. He should have monitored Georgie packing his rucksack, but he'd been too distracted. If they were late that would land Georgie in trouble with Mr Travis, the school coach. 'Can't go back now.'

Georgie shrugged.

Ted felt the guilt kick in. He'd been thinking about meeting Jakob and now Georgie would be running about the freezing pitch in his shorts. They always struggled to get Georgie to wrap up against the cold, so Ted should have remembered to check. 'Will you be able to borrow some?' He knew it was unlikely.

Georgie nodded, but it was just to silence him.

Part of him prayed that Jakob didn't show, or that he'd already been picked up. Terminology that he'd only heard on the news and in crime dramas sprang to mind. Ted was concealing information from a police investigation. Was he aiding and abetting? Ted had been Jakob's friend for over ten years, but did he really owe him this?

But Ted's ultimate goal was to get him to give himself up. Surely the police would understand Ted's motive when Jakob was in custody.

'You're doing it again, Dad.'

Ted checked the road then glanced in the mirror at Georgie's concerned expression. He'd been deep in thought and they were nearly at the park. 'Sorry. Which of your friends is going to be here today?' He knew Jolian and Brendan weren't in the team.

'Just Yash, but he had a bad cold yesterday. His parents probably won't let him come.'

Ted didn't like the idea of Georgie being on his own here. 'It's good to go rogue sometimes though.' He wondered if that was true. He slowed the Corsa and swung it through the green metal gates of the park.

Georgie frowned. 'What does that mean?'

'It means sometimes it's good to do something by yourself.'

'Nobody'll pass me the ball.'

'Then don't wait. Take the ball off them.'

They were both silent as Ted slid the car into a parking space in front of the changing hut. A light rain started falling on the glass.

Ted turned to Georgie. 'I'll be here.' But he wouldn't be. He had to sneak off and meet Jakob on the other side of the park. The coach kept a close eye on them though. How long would his conversation with Jakob take, even if he showed?

'Don't worry, I'll be OK,' Georgie reassured him as he opened his door.

Ted felt a rush of warmth for his son. 'Have fun. See you at half-time.' After he slammed his door, he watched him hitch his rucksack onto his back, even though he would be taking it off a few seconds later, and jog to the changing cabin. Ted scanned the park. A handful of parents were huddled together at the side of the pitch clutching steaming reusable coffee cups. The only other person in sight was a woman walking a red setter down the track on the adjacent side.

He got out, locked the door, zipped up his leather jacket and made his way towards the pavilion.

Chapter 20

Ted strode by the fountain and down the slope towards the cricket pitch and pavilion beyond, his boots squeaking on the overgrown grass. The pavilion was barely a year old. The previous one had nearly collapsed with rot. He'd been inside this one only once, last summer, at its inauguration at the local fair.

He glanced at his watch. It was quarter past eight. There was nobody outside. A stiff breeze drove the cold drizzle at his face. Now a voice told him to call Renton, or maybe ring Juliette first. He prayed Jakob didn't show because, if he did, Ted suspected things would get a lot more complicated.

He halted and looked up at the closed door at the front of the buttermilk panelled wooden building. Was Jakob waiting inside? It was probably locked for the winter though.

Ted continued down to the bottom of the slope and crossed the flat grass and pitch to the three steps that led up to the platform of the pavilion. He climbed them and pushed on the door, but it was locked. Cupping his hand around his eyes he peered in the window. The room was empty except for a table and some rows of stacked green plastic chairs.

'Ted.'

He turned in the direction of the voice and saw Jakob standing at the bottom of the steps. He had no coat and still wore the same dinner party clothes. They were as dishevelled as his expression and his pale-blue shirt was wide open at the collar. His chest rose and fell with heavy breathing.

Jakob beckoned and moved away.

Ted followed him to a bald patch of wet mud littered with cigarette ends, booze bottles and cans at the rear of the pavilion. It was clearly where the kids hung out. Ten feet away was the hedged border of the park and behind that a construction site.

Ted wasn't sure what to say first. 'You look terrible.'

Jakob nodded. 'I feel it.' He swallowed like it was painful. Mud was caked up the arm of one of his shirtsleeves. 'Where's Juliette?' He squinted his red eyes distrustfully.

'At home.'

'You really didn't tell her?' Jakob sounded dubious.

'No.'

Jakob's breath whistled in through his nostrils as he studied him.

'I promise. You asked me not to, but this ...' Ted gestured around them. 'This is as far as it goes. Let me take you to the police now.'

Jakob shook his head and wobbled on his feet, the blood draining from his face.

'Are you OK?'

Jakob stumbled to the back of the pavilion to lean on it and threw up.

Ted watched him finish and spit a few times. 'What happened?' He couldn't delay the question any longer.

Jakob sniffed and wiped moisture from his eyes. 'I really don't know.'

Ted suddenly felt like he'd made a big mistake. 'Come on, me and Juliette found Evie.' He couldn't keep the revulsion from his voice. 'You ran away. What do you expect people to think?'

'I don't know, OK!' Jakob yelled. He inhaled heavily and held his hand up in apology, then lowered his voice again. 'I *really* don't remember. I woke up on the lawn and Evie was lying there ...' Jakob's face twisted up and it looked like he was going to cry. 'And to begin with ... I didn't even know who she was.'

What story was Jakob going to try and feed him?

Jakob's pupils darted as he relived the moment. He wiped some vomit from his lips with the cuff of his shirt. 'I had to rack my brains ...'

Ted remained silent. There was real fear in Jakob's eyes. Was that part of his performance?

'I'm ... I walked back inside the house and heard somebody upstairs. I thought *I* was the intruder. I ran and it felt like I was looking at what was happening through a telescope. Like I was withdrawn from it, just observing. I still feel like it now. It was only later that I remembered.'

'You were fine when you left us, drunk but fine,' Ted reminded him.

'Yes.' He gazed at the ground and frowned. 'I recall getting into the taxi but not much of the journey.'

'What about at home? What happened after you got out of the cab?'

Jakob kept fixated on the butts and bottles. 'We argued.' He shook his head again but this time as if he were trying to dislodge a memory.

'Was it because of the trust game?'

Jakob looked up at him, nodded once. 'I think so.'

'You didn't want to play.' Neither did Ted.

Jakob's face froze as if to channel his energy to recall what happened after. 'That stupid game ...'

'You were getting hostile towards Evie when we played it.'

'This was later, much later. I remember the rage I felt.' Jakob pinched the bridge of his nose as if it would somehow release the moment. 'We were back home but I can't think where.' His right side jerked. 'I think she hit me with something. I've got a huge bruise on the back of my head.' He gingerly touched the area.

'And what then ... you woke on the lawn?'

Jakob nodded, dread like a mask tightening on his face.

'You don't remember attacking her?'

Jakob gulped. 'I never have before. Even during our worst fights.'

The only thing Ted knew for sure was that Jakob's personality changed when he'd drunk too much alcohol.

'I've never struck Evie, never raised a hand to her.' His shoulders rose and fell.

Ted knew his blank expression wasn't what Jakob wanted to see.

'I didn't kill her, Ted. I know I didn't.'

'But you clearly blacked out. Maybe your brain's blocking what you did, I don't know.' This was a Jakob he'd never seen. Four hours after the event and he was still wired, a million miles from the personality Ted sat with at dinner parties.

'I didn't kill her. I'm positive.' The statement was resolute, but Jakob's eyes were full of desperation.

Chapter 21

'Do you remember Evie calling Juliette?' Ted watched Jakob's chest heave.

Jakob flinched, as if it hurt to remember. 'No.'

'That was around four this morning.' But was this all an act? Was Jakob's last defence to feign convenient amnesia?

Jakob shook his head. 'This doesn't happen to me. I lose a few chunks of the evening when I've been drinking but this ...'

'It'll come back.' Ted had to calm him. 'You're not thinking straight. You couldn't have been. Where did you go after you left the house?'

Jakob raised his arms and let them fall again. 'I found myself in Nine Beeches.'

That was the wood behind their property that bordered the east side of Ibbotson. 'You hadn't taken anything?'

'Of course not.' Jakob glared at him, but the intensity quickly waned. 'Haven't for years.'

Ted and Jakob had once shared a joint at a New Year's gathering. That had been more Evie's thing in the past, but neither of them had particularly enjoyed it. 'Come with me back to the car and we can sort this all out.'

Jakob snorted. 'Sort this all out?'

'With the police. It's your only option.' Ted watched Jakob's frame tauten. 'Sooner or later you'll have to. Better to hand yourself over now than be caught.'

'You've told them, haven't you?' Jakob clenched one fist.

'No. If I had, you'd be in custody by now.'

Jakob's eyes darted around them.

'Take a few breaths. You're overwrought.'

Jakob stepped back. 'I need to get my head together first.'

'Where?'

He opened his eyes wide, as if trying to wake himself up. 'Not where I'm going to be interrogated.'

'I'll be there for you, Jakob. Just come with me.' Ted held out his hand.

'I need to know the answers to the questions myself first. Once they have me ...' Jakob recoiled from Ted.

'Then just come back to the car. We can talk before you speak to the police.' But Ted wondered how far his offer really extended. Evie's lifeless and bloodied face was still vivid in his memory.

Jakob seemed to sense his unease and took another pace away from him. 'Just stay there, I'm not going anywhere. And don't tell me that Juliette doesn't know where you are.'

'She doesn't, I promise you. But if she did, she'd be saying the same thing.'

'Liar.' Jakob shot a glance at the border fence.

'Why does her knowing make any difference?'

'This whole thing, the game, that didn't just casually happen.'

'What does that mean?'

'I know how Evie works. She had that ready to go before the evening started.'

'And you're saying Juliette was part of it?'

'The envelopes and paper turned up quickly enough.'

But Ted knew Juliette would instantly be able to locate those. She had a cupboard full of stationery that her mother bought her each year for Christmas that she never used. 'You're being paranoid now. Listen to what you're saying.'

Jakob pressed his palms against his face and rubbed his eyes hard.

'You haven't slept. And you're right: you have to get your head together somewhere. Come with me. Where else can you go?' Jakob didn't have any family in the UK. And from what Juliette had told Ted, he and Evie had very few friends outside of the dinner group.

Jakob's shoulders sagged.

'I'll drive you.' Ted was positive Georgie's coach would drop him home. He wouldn't have him sharing the car with Jakob.

Jakob's eyes were on the middle of Ted's chest.

At that moment, the drizzle, which neither of them had seemed to register during their exchange, turned to hard rain. It was like a full stop to the conversation.

Jakob swayed, blinked, and seemed to withdraw to the night he'd escaped from.

'Jakob?'

His eyes eventually shifted, reluctantly, to Ted's.

'Come on, let's get out of the rain.'

'No,' Jakob said flatly.

'What is it?'

'I need more time.' Jakob immediately started walking towards the border fence at the rear of the pavilion.

'Jakob.' Ted followed. He couldn't let him go. What were the consequences if he did, for both of them? 'Jakob.' He took hold of his elbow.

Jakob swung round and slammed his knuckles into Ted's mouth.

Chapter 22

Ted went down on one knee in the wet mud and put his right hand out to break his fall. His palm slithered and he fell onto his back. He lay there dazed for a few seconds, lip throbbing as the rain fell on his face, and then hinged upright to see Jakob trying to find a gap in the wooden fence. 'Jakob!' He got to his feet but tottered dizzily.

Jakob didn't turn and instead crouched to angle himself through a mass of brambles and ivy that blocked a gap in the lower part of the fence.

'Think about what you're doing!' Ted followed, but the ground tilted under his boots. His lip already felt tight against his teeth.

'Don't come after me! I don't want to hit you again!' Jakob gripped the upper bar of the fence and swung forwards, breaking the creepers with his bulk and dragging his body through.

When Ted reached the fence, he could see Jakob quickly striding across the churned-up clay of the building site. 'Jakob!' But what was the point of pursuing him? He was completely irrational. Ted watched as he darted out of sight behind a dark-blue foreman's hut. Beyond that were gates to a parking area.

He'd certainly proved he was capable of violence. Ted put the pads of his fingers to his lip and examined the blood on them.

He stood there for a few moments, his hair plastered wet to his scalp, his clothes already soaked. Now he had no choice. The sooner Jakob was in custody the better. Was he dangerous? And where was he going? He seemed to think Juliette was partly to blame. Ted called her first and she picked up after three rings.

'Juliette, lock the doors and call the police. I'm on my way home.'

'What's happening?' She sounded breathless. 'Is Georgie all right?'

'Yes, don't worry.' But Ted was already marching back to the slope. 'I've just seen Jakob.'

'Where?'

'Here in the park. I tried to reason with him, but he attacked me and ran off.'

'What? Are you OK?'

'He slugged me. Just a split lip, but I couldn't keep him here.'

'You shouldn't have tried.' There was a brief pause. 'How did he know you'd be there? Did you tell him last night?'

It was time to own up. 'He called me this morning. Told me to keep our meeting a secret, or he wouldn't show.'

Silence.

'He specifically asked me not to tell you.'

'Why?' Her tone had hardened.

He didn't blame Juliette. 'I don't know. Perhaps he thought you'd call the police.'

'Like *you* should have.'

'I wanted to talk sense into him, offered to accompany him to the station. He was behaving like he was on something. I've never seen him like it.'

'What were you thinking?'

'He's been wandering around Nine Beeches. Said he doesn't remember anything about last night.'

'Anything?' She repeated warily. 'And you believe him?'

'We'll talk about this when I get home. He slipped out the fence behind the pavilion. He's running but I don't want to take any chances. Have you double-locked the front door?' Ted trotted up the slope with the phone pressed hard against his ear. He could hear Juliette whispering. 'Who else is there?'

'Kathryn and Rhys. Orla and Connor have just arrived.'

That was a relief. They were obviously rallying around her.

'You're sure Georgie's safe?'

'He's training, other side of the park. Wait ...' Ted reached the top of the slope and looked across the playing field. 'I can see him. I'm going to pull him out of the match and bring him home now.'

'Don't tell him why.'

'Of course not. Call Renton.'

'I'll get Kathryn to do that. I'm staying on the line until you're both in the car.'

'OK.' Ted could hear Juliette relaying the details to Kathryn. He felt a stitch jab him under the rib as he jogged back to the changing hut. 'Wait ... running ... talk in a minute.'

When he got there, he passed the other parents and headed for Mr Travis. Some of the boys turned as he approached, and Georgie met his eye with a frown.

'Sorry. I have to take Georgie home early.' The bearded coach protested but Ted didn't register what he said. 'Family emergency, really sorry about this.' Georgie ran over and Ted took his hand. 'Just grab your bag and you can change in the car.'

They cut across the pitch, puzzlement and disapproval on the faces of the other parents. Or was his split lip more obvious than he thought?

'You've got him?' Juliette asked.

'Yes. All fine,' Ted answered breezily for Georgie's benefit.

'What's happening?' Georgie sounded panicked. 'Who hurt you? Was it the gang?'

Ted knew what Georgie was referring to. A gang had beaten a man to death behind McCoy's nightclub in Basildon a few weeks before and it had been on the local news. Juliette had spent the night trying to get a frightened Georgie to sleep. 'Don't worry, scout. I'll explain when we get home.' But he knew he'd need a story as soon as they were in the car.

'Who are you on the phone to?'

'Your mother's just making sure we're OK.'

'Why wouldn't we be? Is she OK?'

'She's fine.'

'Is it Uncle Jakob?'

Ted slowed his pace and turned to Georgie. 'Why would you say that?'

Georgie looked down at the grass. 'Just wondered.'

'But why?'

Georgie shook his head. 'Is it Grandma then?'

'No.' Ted led them back to the car.

'Grandpa?'

But Ted got the impression that Georgie was covering his tracks. 'I've said I'll explain when we get home. Go and get your rucksack from the changing hut.'

He watched him sprint off. 'Juliette?' Ted knew she would have heard the exchange.

'I'm still here.'

'He seems to know. D'you think he overheard us this morning?' Ted was trying to recall exactly what they'd said during their exchange in the bedroom. But the door had been closed and they hadn't raised their voices.

'He was asleep.'

'He's pretended to be asleep before.' Had Georgie been curious enough about where his parents had gone early in the morning to listen at the door?

Juliette whispered something else away from the phone.

'Juliette?'

'Kathryn's on the phone to the police. Just get Georgie home.'

Chapter 23

Georgie said nothing as they drove out of the park and Ted considered his options. 'What time did you wake up today?'

Georgie frowned at Ted in the mirror.

'Was it just before breakfast?'

His son nodded nervously.

'You weren't awake before that?'

'I don't think so. Who punched you? Was it the gang?'

Ted wiped at his bottom lip and the back of his hand came away streaked with blood. 'No. I'll explain soon. Now, you didn't overhear anything before you got up? I really won't be cross if you did.'

'No. Why?'

Juliette was right. They had to discuss how to break the news to him first. 'It might be a little hard for you to understand.'

'Is it why you took me out of practice?'

'Yes. And I promise we'll talk about it when we get home.'

'OK,' Georgie said, unsure. 'I'm not in trouble?'

'No. I just wondered why you mentioned Uncle Jakob.'

'Is he OK?' Georgie asked innocently.

'He's fine.' Ted accelerated the car through the park gates. 'But we're very concerned about him.'

'Why? Is he ill like Auntie Evie was?'

'No.' Was that it? They'd given him the facts about Evie's cancer when she'd started her treatment and Georgie had become a little obsessed about Uncle Jakob 'catching' the same illness. 'He's not ill like that.'

'Good.' Georgie seemed relieved.

When they pulled up outside home Juliette opened the front door to greet them. She exchanged a glance with Ted as they got out, her face trying not to react to his injury.

Georgie carried his rucksack into the house.

She touched the top of his head. 'Sorry you had to come home early.'

'Somebody hit Dad.' Georgie sounded like he was on the verge of tears.

'I know, we'll fix him up. Go upstairs to your room and play on your Xbox for a bit.'

'He won't tell me who punched him.'

I'll call you down soon.'

'OK,' Georgie complied reluctantly. 'I'll have a shower first.'

Ted heard Georgie greeting the others then thudding upstairs.

Juliette closed the front door behind him, and they walked down the hall. He could see Kathryn, Orla and Connor standing anxiously at the kitchen counter.

'Jesus, that's a belter.' Connor regarded his mouth.

There was a first aid kit open on the chopping board. Juliette started rummaging through it.

'I'm fine.'

'Do you want a painkiller? I've got some strong ones.' Kathryn's eyes were puffy.

So were Orla's. 'He just attacked you?' She flicked her fringe from her lashes.

'Well ... I tried to stop him leaving.' He held up his palm to Juliette as she found a blister pack in the kit.

'Let me take a look.' Juliette squinted at his lip.

'I'm fine ... really.' Ted noticed somebody missing. 'Rhys not here?'

'He was. But he had to pick the girls up from their sleepover,' Kathryn answered, vaguely.

'The police?'

Juliette nodded at Ted. 'Renton's coming over.'

'Shall I see if he's OK?' Ted rolled his eyes to the ceiling.

'What did you tell him?' Juliette whispered.

'As little as possible. He knows something bad is going on though.'

'Jakob must be possessed.' Connor shook his head.

'What exactly happened?' Orla croaked; her features even paler than usual.

Ted recounted the events at the park.

'They'll have him soon,' Kathryn said stolidly.

Ted pulled a chair from the table. He realized it was the seat Evie had sat in only eight hours before. He dragged the next one out and dropped into it. Among the bottles and remaining dinner debris in front of him was the yellow ashtray, its interior still blackened with burnt secrets.

Chapter 24

'I still can't shake the idea that if we hadn't played Evie's trust game ...'

Nobody responded to Ted.

He turned to the other four, but none of them made eye contact. Had they held this discussion already? 'We should tell Renton.'

Juliette walked to the kettle. 'I thought we'd talked about this.' She clicked it on.

Ted studied Kathryn, Orla and Connor. Connor wrung his fingers awkwardly. The other two were motionless.

'I'm making more coffee,' Juliette stated.

'We should have told him earlier.' Ted followed Juliette's gaze to the others.

'I'll have another cup.' Kathryn nodded to her empty one on the counter.

'So it's been decided.'

Juliette sighed. 'Nothing's been decided. We don't know what happened between them, but if it was anything to do with Evie's game ...'

'Yes?' He held her eye.

'Then Jakob must have been pretty unstable,' Orla interjected, her tone hostile.

Ted was taken aback. She'd never spoken to him like that before. Her passive aggression was usually reserved for Connor.

'I think we're attaching too much importance to it,' Kathryn mitigated, sliding her cup down the counter to the kettle so that she didn't have to look at Ted.

'Perhaps you're right.' Ted raised his voice as the kettle started to grumble. 'So why don't we tell Renton exactly what happened?'

'It would only complicate matters.' Kathryn sniffed.

Ted could see how the conversation was going. 'For whom?'

'We all played it.' Connor folded his arms.

'But none of us would have, if we'd known this was going to happen.'

'Please ...' Kathryn held up her hand to Ted but still didn't look at him. 'Stop insinuating that we were to blame.'

Ted took a breath. Everyone was broken up by what had happened and here he was suggesting they might be responsible. 'There were obviously things going on between Evie and Jakob that we didn't know about. All I'm saying is that Jakob's mood changed after we played the trust game.' He realized that wasn't helping and tried a different tack. 'We all know Jakob gets a bit more ... animated after a few glasses of wine.'

Kathryn kept her attention on the counter.

'Which is why none of us gave the game another thought when we went to bed.' But the lack of agreement in the room said that wasn't true. 'We're all traumatized by this, none of us is thinking clearly. We all had plenty to drink ...'

'I've never felt as sober.' Orla absently played with her wedding ring.

'I'm feeling nauseous.' Kathryn closed her eyes and inhaled. 'And I'm having a hot flush.'

'D'you need some fresh air?' Juliette indicated the kitchen window.

'I'll be fine in a minute.' Kathryn shuffled over to the table and dropped heavily into a chair.

Juliette opened the window then grabbed a tumbler and filled it with cold water.

'I think we're *all* feeling the same.' Ted picked up on Juliette's glare as she shook her head at him.

She took the water over to Kathryn.

Connor went to the other side of the table and sat down. Orla drifted to the window behind it and looked blankly into the back yard.

Four of them stared at the ashtray.

Ted couldn't let it go. 'If we're all having reservations about it, we can't omit it from our account of the evening.'

'Ted,' Juliette remonstrated and sat down next to Kathryn.

'I was meant to be seeing Evie again on Thursday,' Orla

said to the pane. 'I should call and cancel the reservation.' She distractedly rubbed her tattooed arms.

Kathryn took a large gulp of her water.

'OK?' Juliette placed her hand on hers.

Kathryn nodded but Ted could see her usually flushed complexion was white. The bun that she'd worn tight on her head the night before had half unravelled.

Connor ran his fingers along the edge of his place mat. 'Maybe they've already picked Jakob up. He's the only one who knows what really happened. Perhaps we're worrying about a conversation we don't need to have.'

But Ted knew none of them believed that would be the case.

'Excuse me.' Kathryn got up and rushed in the direction of the bathroom. She banged the door after her.

The kettle boiled and clicked and as the bubbles subsided the room was unnervingly silent.

Chapter 25

L ess than a minute later, the doorbell rang.
'I'll get it.' Ted was first to his feet. When he opened the front door, he found Renton standing outside with a tall, male plain-clothes officer. 'Come in.'

Renton remained motionless for a moment, fixing Ted's split lip with disapproval, before stepping inside. 'This is Detective Sergeant Patterson.' He jerked his thumb at his companion.

He was slight, mid-thirties, in a blue mackintosh with obviously dyed black hair shaved close to the tops of his ears.

'Come through.' Ted led them down the hallway to the dining room, and as they entered a mumbled conversation ceased.

Juliette and Connor rose from their chairs.

'I don't mean to intrude on ... your gathering.' Renton took off his fur hunting hat and wiped a strand of dark hair across his bald scalp.

'This is Orla and Connor Lowney,' Juliette introduced them.

Connor dipped his head, and Orla turned slowly from the window.

Juliette cleared her throat. 'Our friend Kathryn Driscoll is here too. She's just ... in the bathroom.'

'The people you were with last night?' Renton checked his watch. 'They're staying with you then?'

'No.' Juliette guessed why he would be asking. 'They all live locally. They came over when they heard the news.'

Renton pursed his lips. 'You informed them?'

Juliette nodded. 'I hope that was OK.'

Renton didn't respond but glanced at his colleague. Then he took in the table and the empty wine bottles. 'Looks like you had quite the festive evening. A celebration?'

Ted felt protective of Juliette and moved past the two police officers to stand beside her. 'Just a get-together.'

'You all took taxis home?'

'Yes,' Connor replied brusquely.

Renton's pockmarked expression remained impassive. He swivelled to Ted. 'Is there somewhere private we can talk?'

Ted guessed why he was being asked. 'Yes, this way.' He gestured Renton out of the dining room and towards the lounge.

Juliette followed but Renton held out his hand. 'Just your husband first, if that's OK.'

She froze and swapped a worried look with Ted as he escorted them out.

* * *

Renton closed the door behind the three of them. 'Do you have any idea how severe the consequences could be for what you did this morning?'

'I'm sorry. Jakob called when we got back from Ibbotson. He said if I involved the police he wouldn't show. I wanted to talk him into giving himself up, but when he refused I phoned you straight away.'

'Mrs Middleton phoned.'

'I asked her to.'

'Why didn't you immediately call us?' Renton undid his woollen overcoat to reveal a mustard shirt one size too small for his paunch.

'I was worried about her being here alone, so I rang her first.'

'You thought Mr Eriksson was a threat to her?'

'He wasn't in his right mind. I've never seen him like it.'

'But why would you think he'd endanger your wife and son?'

'I took my son, Georgie, to the park with me.' Ted reacted to Renton's frown. 'I do every Saturday for football practice. Jakob arranged to meet me by the pavilion after I'd dropped him off.'

'You took your son along to meet the man who very probably murdered his wife?' Renton said incredulously.

'I dropped Georgie off with his coach and then walked to the other side of the park to meet Jakob at the pavilion.'

Detective Sergeant Patterson took out his iPhone and started tapping the screen.

Renton continued. 'So why would Jakob attack your wife?'

'I wasn't convinced of that ... just concerned.' But how could he tell him that Jakob was suspicious of Juliette's participation in a game that he hadn't yet disclosed? He had to convince the others to tell Renton; he couldn't do it like this. 'Jakob seemed like he was wired, like he'd taken something.'

'You've seen him like that before? Like he's taken something?' Renton squinted.

'No.' Except for that New Year's Eve, when they'd shared a joint. But neither of them had been that affected.

'So why would you think he'd come here? Had Mrs Middleton quarrelled with him?'

'No.'

'Had they had any grievances in the past?'

'No,' Ted said categorically.

'Then why?'

'He gave me this, when I tried to help him.' He indicated his split lip.

Renton didn't look at it. 'I was coming to that, but you still haven't answered my question.'

'I rang her to explain what had happened and suggested she lock the door.'

'So, she was waiting for the outcome of your meeting with Mr Eriksson?'

'No, she didn't know I was meeting him.'

Renton's frown deepened. 'Why didn't you tell her?'

'He told me not to tell anyone.'

Renton filled his chest. 'And when he hit you, that's when you decided to tell her?'

'Yes.'

'But if she had your friends here for company you shouldn't have been that nervous about Jakob paying her a visit.'

'I didn't know they were here.'

'When did they arrive then? After you left for football practice?'

'Yes. She broke the news and they came round.'

'Or did she invite them?'

'No.' But Ted wasn't sure. 'Ask Juliette. I've only just got back myself.'

Renton chewed his lip for a moment. 'I'm going to be blunt because I need to know exactly why Mr Eriksson is behaving the way he is. You're not aware of any sort of relationship between Mr Eriksson and your wife that would make you think he'd head over here to harm her?'

'No.' Ted waited for Renton to blink. He didn't.

The other detective looked up from his phone then returned his attention to the screen.

'And you're not withholding anything from me, for your wife's sake?'

Ted tried not to tense. 'No.' Had Renton's suspicions been aroused when he'd first interviewed them? 'There is no relationship,' he added.

'I'd advise a rethink, if you are. You've already prevented

me from bringing Mr Eriksson in. That means you could be liable for endangering others.'

'I'm not.' Juliette having a relationship with Jakob was as absurd as him being violent towards Evie.

'Are you going to put some ice on that?' Renton studied Ted's lip.

Chapter 26

After Ted had outlined the specifics of his meeting with Jakob, Renton waited while Detective Sergeant Patterson finished inputting the information into the notebook on his phone.

Ted filled the silence. 'Like I said, after he slugged me, I was pretty dazed.'

Renton grunted as he loosened his shirt collar. 'And you said nothing that triggered his attack?'

'No. Just tried to restrain him.'

'He claimed he had absolutely no recollection of what happened to Mrs Eriksson?'

'Just those brief flashes of being at home.'

'You believe him?'

Ted didn't know how to respond. 'It sounds ... unlikely.' Ted felt a pang of guilt, but that was what he thought.

'Let's join the others.' Renton pointed to the door.

Ted opened it and they walked back to the dining room. Kathryn had rejoined Juliette, Orla and Connor and they were all sitting at the table. Ted noticed the empty wine bottles and glasses had been cleared away. The ashtray too.

Juliette tried to read Ted's expression. 'OK?'

Ted nodded.

Juliette stood. 'This is Kathryn Driscoll.'

Kathryn got to her feet and turned towards them. Her face was ashen.

Renton tightened his lips at her. 'So we're missing one.'

He had obviously taken note of the names Ted had given him that morning in Ibbotson.

'Yes. My husband, Rhys,' Kathryn replied. 'He's gone to get our girls from a sleepover.'

'And then he'll be on his way here?'

'Just to pick me up. He was actually here earlier.'

'So you've all spoken?' Renton darted his dark eyes to each of them.

They nodded.

Renton waited for his colleague to finish making a note.

'Can I make you some coffee?' Juliette offered.

'No, thanks. So what time did the party finish?' Renton aimed the question at Orla.

She shifted uncomfortably in her seat, glanced at Connor and then wiped her fringe from her eyes. 'We all left around the same time, about one-ish?' She looked to Juliette for confirmation.

'Yes.' Juliette agreed. 'We usually call the cabs around that time.'

'I can give you the number of the firm we used,' Ted

suggested. 'It's on the door of the freezer. Maybe their driver overheard something.'

'Maybe.' Renton turned to his colleague and Detective Sergeant Patterson crossed the room to note it down. 'So Mr Eriksson was drunk?'

'We'd all had enough but nobody was motherless,' Connor answered, his Northern Irish accent suddenly thick.

'Motherless?' Renton frowned.

'So drunk you can't remember who your mother is.' Connor smiled humourlessly. 'Nobody was in that much of a state.'

'And wine was the strongest thing available to Mr Eriksson?'

Ted figured what he was digging around for. 'There were no drugs.'

'There was an ashtray on the table when I came in.'

The atmosphere tightened.

'We don't have drugs in the house,' Juliette said emphatically.

Ted knew that hadn't always been strictly true, but since Georgie it had definitely been the case.

'Nobody was smoking anything illegal?'

'No,' Kathryn reacted, mortified.

Ted realized it was genuine. Kathryn and Rhys had joined the dinner party group long after the days of the odd joint at the back door.

'Mr Eriksson told Mr Middleton that he remembers

very little before waking on the lawn beside the body of his wife.'

Everyone around the table turned their gaze to Ted.

'I just want to establish if it was because of something he'd taken here.'

'No,' Ted enunciated.

Renton regarded him with suspicion. 'Nothing he might have taken in private in the bathroom?'

Ted shook his head.

'You've never seen him indulge in anything like that?'

Ted hesitated.

'I'm not looking to press drugs charges, Mr Middleton. Just tell me what happened.'

'Look, we'll all take a test, if that's what you need. But there were absolutely no drugs taken here last night.'

Renton grinned at Juliette's assurance. 'Nothing taken here last night.' He said aloud to his colleague.

Detective Sergeant Patterson tapped the screen of his phone.

Chapter 27

'So you wouldn't say Mr Eriksson was any drunker than the rest of you?' Renton returned his attention to Kathryn.

She shook her head. 'After a few glasses he can often get ... spirited.'

'Spirited. In what way? Do you mean aggressive?'

'No, not physically aggressive.'

'Verbally? Have you seen that in the past?'

Kathryn considered it. 'No.'

'You had to think about that.'

'I meant he just comes out of his shell, gets a bit more opinionated.' The edges of Kathryn's mouth trembled.

'So nobody was aware of any significant issue between Mr and Mrs Eriksson?'

Everyone shook their heads.

'No?' Renton asked it directly of Orla.

'No,' Connor responded harshly.

Now was the opportune time for Ted to inform Renton about the trust game. They had nothing to hide, but it was Juliette's reluctance that troubled him most. Was she afraid that they'd have to reveal what they'd written down? Was her secret that bad? But they could all lie about them now. Only Evie's and Jakob's might throw some light on what happened.

Kathryn turned her chair around and sat down again. 'They had some problems a few years ago and briefly went to a therapist.'

'Any idea what that was about?'

'Yes,' Juliette replied flatly.

Ted had noticed that Renton hadn't asked any questions of her.

She obviously had as well. 'They couldn't have children. It caused some friction, but they moved past it. That's all we know.'

'We?' Renton repeated.

Juliette tightened her jaw.

'You're speaking for everybody here now?'

'No.' Juliette blinked hard. 'We all know that.'

'Do you?' He studied the others and then focused on Ted.

Ted nodded.

'So nobody has any idea about what may have sparked such aggression between the two of them last night?'

'No,' Connor answered immediately. 'And I really don't understand why you're interrogating us like this.'

'I've got men searching for Mr Eriksson, but while that's happening, I'm just trying to understand his frame of mind when he left here. So Mr and Mrs Eriksson's marriage had recovered, and they were happy again.'

'As happy as they could be.' Connor shrugged.

'What does that mean?' Renton came to the table and sat down.

Ted knew that everyone was thinking the same thing: Renton was seated in Evie's chair, the one they'd all avoided.

'They're married; I'm saying happiness is relative,' Connor said sardonically.

'Connor,' Orla warned. 'You're not helping.'

Renton didn't appear amused. He interlinked his stubby, hairy fingers on the tabletop. 'Did they often go to Nine Beeches?' He looked up at Ted.

'Not that I know of. It's just the forest that borders their neighbourhood. I suppose Jakob ended up there after he left their house.'

'I've sent a car over. He didn't say how long he was in there?'

'He told me he didn't know how he got there.' Ted recalled how flipped out he'd been. Had it really been an act?

'Anywhere else you think he'd go?'

'If he's innocent, he would've already given himself up.' Kathryn took a tissue from her sleeve.

'Where did he work?'

'St Ballantine's Primary. Same place as Evie.' Juliette rubbed her eyes.

'Surely he wouldn't go to his school,' said Connor.

'It'll be empty today.' Ted realized with some relief.

'Might be a reason for him to go. I'd better post someone there.' Renton signalled his colleague.

Detective Sergeant Patterson started making the call and strode into the hall.

Chapter 28

'Thanks for the offer of the coffee.' Renton pulled his black hunting hat on and took stock of the faces around the table. 'I'll leave you in peace now, but I may want to talk to each of you again.' His gaze lingered on Juliette. 'We'll let ourselves out.' He gestured to his colleague and they thumped towards the front door.

Juliette took a pace after them. 'You'll let us know as soon as you find Jakob?'

'Of course. If he tries to make contact with anyone here, you let me know immediately.' He raised his eyebrows at Ted.

'We will,' Juliette answered for him.

Connor waited for the door to click shut behind them, before he addressed Ted. 'What did he say to you in there?'

'Balled me out for not telling him about meeting Jakob.'

'You didn't tell him about Evie's game?' Orla sounded fearful.

'No.'

'Sounds like he's more interested in charging us with drug possession.' Kathryn shook her head.

'That's because I told him Jakob was out of it.'

Connor folded his arms. 'He really enjoyed making us all uncomfortable, didn't he?'

'D'you think we'll see him again?' Orla seemed to dread the idea.

Connor puffed his cheeks. 'Depends on what Jakob says.'

'And what if he says it was all down to Evie's party game? We still haven't told him about it,' Ted reminded them all.

'He was too busy making insinuations to give us a chance.' Kathryn dabbed at her nose with a fresh tissue.

But Ted knew it was an excuse. 'If he wants detailed statements about the evening, we tell him. Agreed?'

'It was Evie's idea,' Kathryn said, nettled.

'Which is why none of us should have a problem with it.'

'OK, if he comes back to us again we tell him.' Juliette barely restrained her temper.

'It's the right thing to do.' Ted locked eyes with her. He could feel the discomfort of the others.

Juliette nodded, her enmity wavering.

Connor broke the atmosphere. 'Ted's right, we have to get it into perspective. We've done nothing wrong. We're all just feeling a bit ... dislocated by what's happened.'

The doorbell rang and everyone's focus shifted to the hall.

'Probably Rhys,' Kathryn said, unsure.

Ted got up, strode to the front door and recognized Rhys's outline outside the glass. He opened it.

Rhys regarded Ted's injury and sucked air in through his lips. 'Nasty.'

'I'm fine.'

'Any news?' He was out of breath. 'I just saw the police car.' But Rhys didn't step in.

'No sign of Jakob.' He registered that the portion of face visible above Rhys's beard was flushed bright red.

'How was he when you saw him?'

Ted beckoned him inside.

'Can't. Girls are in the car.'

'Said he couldn't remember anything about what happened.'

'Nothing?' Rhys said incredulously.

'He was manic. I tried to get him to come with me to the police and that's when he turned on me. Are you all right?'

Rhys gulped and wet his lips. 'Fine. Just wanted to get back here as soon as I could and find out what happened.'

'I'll fill you in.' Kathryn had appeared beside Ted. 'We'll leave you in peace, Ted. Phone us if you have any news.' She slipped past him, pulling her teal cashmere shawl on.

'Take care,' Rhys said. 'Speak soon.' He held Ted's eye for a moment and then followed his wife down the path.

Ted turned when he heard more footsteps. Orla and Connor were tugging their coats off the banister in the hallway.

'We'll be on our way as well. Orla's not feeling too good.' Connor wound his scarf around his neck.

Juliette was with them. 'You probably need some rest.'

Ted wondered if Orla would be taking her super-strength

pills to help her sleep. He was sure they'd all be struggling with that though.

They said goodbye and Orla shuffled past without a word. She looked so pale and fragile and Connor put his arm around her waist as she walked unsteadily down the path. Ted felt Juliette's hand on his shoulder as she joined him to watch them go.

None of them looked back as they headed to their cars.

Chapter 29

Neither of them said anything until they'd walked back into the dining room.

'I'll load the dishwasher.' Juliette headed towards the kitchen area.

'Hang on a minute. Are you OK?'

'Of course not. But what else can we do?'

'Ever since we drove to Evie and Jakob's ...'

She regarded him with strained mystification.

'You're acting as if ... you're behaving strangely.'

Her expression hardened. 'And how am I meant to be behaving?'

'All we did was throw a dinner party. Evie wanted to play that game and we all went along with it, some more willingly than others.'

'You mean I was more willing than you.'

'No, that's not important.'

'But you just made that distinction. That leaves you less to blame than me. Is that why you're so comfortable telling the police about it?'

'The most important thing is telling the truth.'

Juliette breathed in and paused as if considering something. 'OK, I'll be honest.' The hostility was back in her voice. 'I'd rather Renton didn't know because I feel terrible that we might have contributed to what happened. Can you understand that?'

'Yes, but I think, if it's out in the open, we'll all feel better about it.'

'Well, you may get your wish. If we're all interrogated again, we've agreed we'll tell. Then your conscience will be clear, clearer than mine.'

'It did change the atmosphere around the table.'

'And us?'

'Us as well.'

'So, you need to know what I wrote down, is that it?'

'No.' Ted responded too quickly.

'Because you don't want to tell me what was written on yours.'

'I will, if that's important.' But Ted realized that would be the price of getting the answer he needed. And could their day withstand any more trauma?

'No, what's important right now is that Evie is dead, and her husband is responsible.'

'I'm sorry.' He knew he needed to step back.

'These conversations are not for today. Maybe sometime soon we can talk about you keeping your meeting with Jakob a secret from me too.'

'He told me not to. Otherwise I wouldn't have had a chance to talk him into going to the police with me.'

Juliette shook her head for him to stop.

'I thought I was doing the right thing.'

Juliette opened her mouth but bit her lip.

Ted could see the distress deep in her eyes. They'd both been through a lot in the past six hours.

'Can we please just wait to see what happens when they find Jakob?'

He nodded. 'Yes. Of course. I'm sure that won't be long.' Did their relief really hinge on the arrest of their friend?

'Let's get tidied up in the meantime. Then we have to discuss what to tell Georgie.'

'OK.' He knew this was her usual coping mechanism, a list of jobs to do. He'd seen it go into overdrive when her father died.

He helped her load the remaining glasses and plates into the dishwasher and noticed she'd already cleaned the ashtray in the sink. It was lying pristine on the draining board.

Chapter 30

When the phone awoke Ted his bedside clock said it was 5.27. He scrabbled for the handset in the dark and quickly answered.

'Mr Middleton?'

Renton's voice slid the events of the last day heavily into his stomach. 'Yes?' He sat up and waited to feel Juliette stir beside him. 'What is it?' He swung his legs off the bed.

'Are you OK to talk?' Renton had obviously picked up on his cracked voice.

What a dumb thing to say so early in the morning. But then Ted realized he was still fully clothed, and the curtains were open. It was dark outside, but it was only half five on Saturday afternoon. He'd tried to catch up on some sleep and had been out for less than an hour.

'We've found Mr Eriksson.'

'You have?' Relief slowed his heart. 'Is he OK?'

'I'm afraid it's bad news.'

Ted held his breath and waited for Renton to continue.

'It looks like suicide.'

'What?' his mouth asked while his brain grappled with the news.

'An officer found him hanging from a tree in Nine Beeches.'

Ted shook his head. 'When?' It was a pointless question.

'Just over an hour ago.'

Ted squinted at the empty bed beside him. Juliette had told him to get some rest, while she spent some time with Georgie in his room before they both spoke to him about his Auntie Evie. Her death hadn't even sunk in. What would they tell their son now?

'I'm sorry,' Renton said, stilted, like he was reading from a script.

Ted hardly heard him. He was already contemplating what the news meant. His friend was dead. An intelligent, generous man he'd known for over a decade was hanging lifelessly from a tree. Inevitable questions crowded in: what would have happened if he hadn't let him go? What if he'd tried harder to restrain him?

'Mr Middleton?'

Ted suddenly felt freezing. 'I'm here.'

'I realize this is a shock, but I need a definite answer.'

Ted waited for him to elaborate, but he didn't. What was he talking about?

'In the absence of his wife identifying the body we need someone else to confirm that it's him.'

Having only had seconds to digest this horrible news

he was being asked to ... He tried to think of other people who might have been closer to Jakob.

'You mentioned he doesn't have any family here.'

'No.' A dizzying nausea fizzed through his scalp.

'Obviously, if we had to, we could try to contact one of his fellow teachers at the school.'

But Ted had heard all about the petty politics that went on there, and Jakob had little good to say about his colleagues.

'Maybe you have a number for someone you think is more appropriate.'

There wasn't, and Renton knew it. Besides, Ted wasn't comfortable with passing this along. He was the last person to see him alive, but more importantly, he *was* his friend. Even though every cell of him didn't want to see Jakob in a morgue, he had to do it.

'Mr Middleton?'

'When do you need me to come down there?' Ted heard himself say.

'What are your plans now?'

Now? Ted swallowed a hard ball of nothing. He'd scarcely woken up.

'His body will be transported to County Hall in Chelmsford by seven tonight.'

Chelmsford? That was about eighteen miles away. He tried to focus on the details and not to think of Jakob as the body in question.

'That should give you time.'

Time? Ted was still lost for words.

'I'd be very grateful, Mr Middleton.' But there wasn't a trace of gratitude in his voice.

'I'll be there at seven.' Ted cut the call and remained where he was, listening to the silent house. He wanted to stay hunkered in the darkness. Not add worse news to what Juliette and Georgie were already dealing with. He breathed in a few times, listened to the blood throbbing in his temples and then went slowly to the door.

Chapter 31

Ted was glad of the satnav as he negotiated his blue Corsa through Chelmsford's high street and into Victoria Road. How was he meant to feel about identifying his friend? Whether or not it was an accident, Jakob had killed Evie and changed from the person he'd known for so long into the stranger he'd met in the park.

He had to remind himself what time of day it was. The city was busy with people going out for the evening. Laughing, joking, looking forward to a drink and a meal and briefly forgetting life's worries, as he had been the night before.

'At the roundabout take the third exit,' the robotic female voice advised him.

He obeyed. Ted had to get back home as soon as possible. When he'd gone downstairs to break the news he'd found Juliette and Georgie on the couch watching something on Netflix. She'd been staring through the TV with her hand stroking his head. He'd called her out of the room and taken her into the front lounge.

He hadn't wanted to tell her in the kitchen, where the dining table was.

Ted couldn't recall her facial reaction. They'd said hardly anything to each other, partly because they didn't want Georgie overhearing them. She was horrified that he had to identify the body. But she'd taken as long as he had to realize that there was nobody else.

Now they both had to work out a way to explain what had happened and they had only tomorrow to sit Georgie down. Doubtless it would be in the news by the time he went back to school, so it had to come from them.

Ted pulled into the County Hall forecourt and found only a handful of vehicles there. He switched off the engine but didn't move from the driving seat. It was just gone five to seven. The quicker he went in the quicker he could be away, but he was sure he'd be coming out a different person. Until Evie he'd only ever seen one dead person in his life and that was his grandmother at her open-casket funeral. But she'd been ninety-eight, and the embalmer had made her look content with the years she'd had. Jakob was his age, thirty-five, and he couldn't imagine how distressed he'd been as he'd choked and jerked on a rope as he'd died alone in Nine Beeches.

He got out of the car and counted the six steps as he climbed them to the main entrance. Pushing the stiff door, he was relieved to find Renton waiting for him.

He stood up from the coffee machine and indicated the small brown cup in his hand. 'Can I get you one?'

Ted shook his head.

Renton nodded, sensing how tense he was. 'OK, let's get this done.'

Sound echoed off the empty corridor walls, as Renton led him to the rear of the building and then down a flight of steps, through some double doors and into a wall of pungent septic aroma.

'If you'd just wait here.'

After Renton exited through another set of doors, Ted examined the anteroom he was standing in. It was vacant except for a row of four orange plastic chairs against the mint green wall in front of him. He turned and his stomach shuddered at what was behind him. The top half of the wall was glass and beyond the pane was a table with a bagged body on it.

The dark-blue plastic had a sticker with a serial number attached to the body's waist. He anticipated the swing door behind it opening but there was no sign of movement.

That was Jakob lying there. Ted absently sucked at the lump on his lip. It had barely started to heal from that morning, but the fist that had caused it was now cold and zipped away.

He waited for what felt like minutes. Was Renton doing this on purpose? Eventually the door opened and a woman in her thirties entered, wearing a plastic green apron and with her dark hair tied in a ponytail. She didn't look at him but approached the table and very deliberately unzipped the top of the bag with her surgically gloved fingers.

As soon as Jakob's face was exposed Ted felt his insides begin to shrivel. The whole head was dark purple, the protruding eyes wide, almost as if the pressure around his neck had pushed the lids permanently open. But there was no expression. It was empty; dead flesh no longer occupied by the man he'd known.

Ted registered the woman was waiting for his response. He briefly met her eye and nodded. Then nodded again so she would be in no doubt and could zip away the face.

She did and then slowly left the room.

Ted turned away and Renton entered a few moments later.

'Do you need to sit down?'

Ted shook his head.

'Don't mind if I do?' Renton gestured to a chair.

Ted shrugged while Renton sat.

He interlinked his stubby fingers in his lap and looked up at Ted. 'He left no message, if that's what you're thinking.'

He wasn't. Should he have? But it was no surprise; Jakob had been out of control.

'I've just heard his sister is flying out this evening. Do you know if Mr Eriksson had any financial issues?'

'He was a teacher. I think he and Evie had their fair share, but I wasn't aware of anything major.'

'He didn't confide in you about anything like that?'

'No.' Ted didn't want to be in the room any longer.

'Can often be the case. Somebody suppresses their

problems day in, day out and all it takes is that one extra nudge to push them over the edge.'

'I really don't know.' The chemical smell seemed to get stronger.

Renton nodded. 'OK. There'll be an autopsy so we can find out exactly what he had in his system. You think he may have taken something?'

'It did seem that way.'

'Something that he must have taken when he got home, immediately *after* he'd been with his friends for the entire evening.'

Ted noted the cynicism in his voice. 'Yes. He may have been drunk when he left us, but he was still the Jakob I knew.'

'And he wasn't in the park?'

'No.' Ted tried to keep his temper in check. 'Can I go now? I need to be with my wife.'

'Yes, of course.' Renton remained seated. 'Go and discuss it with her. I'll be in touch presently.'

Chapter 32

When Ted walked into the hallway, Juliette came down the stairs. She paused on the last one, expression on hold, and remained there while Ted closed the door and hung up his jacket.

'Are you OK?' she whispered.

Ted walked up the hallway to her. He'd felt numb for the entire journey home, awaiting an emotional reaction that hadn't come. 'Georgie in bed?' he whispered.

Juliette looked briefly back up the stairs and nodded once, lips tightly sealed.

'They're doing an autopsy to find out if he'd taken something.' Ted kept his voice low. 'There was no note, but I didn't think there would be.'

Juliette's eyes briefly darted. 'Nothing at all?'

'No. So now we'll never really know what happened.'

Juliette sat on the third step from the bottom.

'Are *you* OK?'

He joined her there.

She dipped her head forward, short grey bob hanging

over her face. 'I'll be fine. I just had to tell Georgie.'

Ted frowned. 'I thought we were going to wait until I got back.'

She looked up again. 'He kept asking what was going on. Where you'd gone. I couldn't lie to him.'

'What did you say?'

'That there was a terrible row, that his uncle got too angry and his auntie got badly hurt. So hurt that she'd have to have a funeral like his grandad. And that Uncle Jakob was so sad about what he'd done that he wanted to be in the same place.'

Ted recalled the chat they'd had with him before Juliette's father's funeral. He'd found refuge from the uncomfortable conversation by playing with his toys.

'He didn't speak when I was getting him ready for bed. He said he wanted to have another shower and he's only just come out.'

Ted offered her his hand. 'Let's go.'

She took it and her fingers were freezing.

Ted led her into the lounge, and she sat on the couch. A cartoon was on with the sound turned down. He arranged the TV blanket around her. 'I'll go and see Georgie and then make us coffee.'

'We haven't eaten all day.' But it was only a statement.

Ted was positive neither of them would be having dinner. 'What about Georgie?'

'He had some pizza earlier.' Juliette stared through the screen.

Ted went upstairs to Georgie's room. As he entered his son hurriedly arranged the duvet over his legs. He'd obviously been listening at the door and jumped in when he heard Ted coming. 'OK, scout?'

He nodded his mess of wet hair.

That was unlike Georgie. He enjoyed repeatedly combing it in the mirror. 'You should use the hair dryer before you go to sleep.' But Ted could tell he wasn't tired. 'As it's Saturday though, maybe you can catch up on some screen time first.'

Georgie half-smiled for his benefit but made no move to grab his tablet from the table beside him.

Ted seated himself on the edge of the bed. 'Have you been thinking about Auntie Evie and Uncle Jakob?'

He nodded again.

'I feel a bit sick thinking about it. Is that how you feel?'

Georgie looked up. 'When *you* both argue ...'

Ted could see the fear in his eyes. 'No. Listen, we argue sometimes, like you do with your friends, but we always make up. It's the rule.'

'You promise?'

'I promise,' Ted said resolutely.

Georgie didn't look convinced. 'Do you swear on your mother's life?'

Ted swallowed. 'We don't do that.' But he knew his son might have heard Connor say that in the past. Georgie had obviously done his share of eavesdropping during their get-togethers downstairs.

141

'But if you're telling the truth, why wouldn't you?'

'Because it's not a nice thing to say. A personal promise is enough. You're nothing if you're not as good as your word.'

Georgie thought about that.

'Do you think I'm as good as my word?'

'You *did* say you'd clear out the garage as a den.'

'And I will. Because I promised. But first I promise that what happened to Auntie Evie and Uncle Jakob will never happen in this house. Do you believe me?'

'Is that cos you're not an issue like Uncle Jakob?'

Ted assumed that Georgie was again using a word he might have overheard. 'I think Uncle Jakob might have had some "issues" but that's a little more complicated to explain. We can talk about that another time.'

Georgie seemed confused. 'But I thought Uncle Jakob was an issue. What is an issue then?'

'Who said Uncle Jakob was an issue?'

Georgie looked sheepish.

'Were you listening when you shouldn't have been?' Ted began to scour his recent conversations. 'If you've heard anything today that you don't understand then just ask me and I'll explain.'

'No, this was last week when Auntie Evie was here.'

'At this house?' But only the day before Juliette had said she hadn't seen Evie and Jakob since May. And hadn't they all reiterated that at the dinner party? 'Are you sure?'

'She came round after I got picked up from Peta's.'

'And Uncle Jakob wasn't here?'

'No.'

'Which day?'

'Tuesday, I think. That's when I heard Auntie Evie say he was an issue.'

Chapter 33

Ted confirmed with Georgie that Evie had been speaking in the kitchen with Juliette the previous Tuesday evening. That was the night he'd had leaving drinks with a colleague. 'How long did Auntie Evie stay for?'

Georgie shrugged. 'Not very long.'

'And did you hear her say anything else?'

He shook his head but looked down at his SpongeBob duvet cover.

'I'm not angry if you were listening.' Which wasn't consistent with the chat they'd had with him about eavesdropping. 'Not on this occasion. Just think back to what she might have said.' Why hadn't Juliette told him?

'That was it. Auntie Evie sounded upset and said Uncle Jakob was an issue. I didn't listen to anymore. I thought they might be secretly talking about my birthday party.'

Ted understood why he would lose interest once he'd established they weren't. 'So Auntie Evie didn't come in to say hello to you?'

'No. She went out the back door.'

The Dinner Party

Why had Evie come over, flustered, three days before the dinner party and then acted as if she hadn't seen them for eight months? He tried to replay the conversation when she'd arrived with Jakob on Friday. Had Ted just assumed she hadn't been there recently, because he'd been out when she'd called in on Tuesday? But surely Juliette would have mentioned it to him, particularly if Evie had been emotional. 'So you don't remember anything else?'

He shook his head again and seemed nervous of Ted's expression. 'Am I in trouble now?'

'No, of course not. Dry your hair and I'll be in to turn out your light. Screen time until half eight, OK?'

Georgie brightened at that.

Ted closed the door after him and went back downstairs. How would he broach asking Juliette about Evie's visit? It appeared Jakob was oblivious to the meeting as well. He'd needed prompting about the last time they'd all got together. Why was he an 'issue'?

But when Ted walked into the lounge, Juliette was asleep, her face on the arm of the couch and the TV blanket pulled up under her chin.

He stepped quietly to the kitchen to make the coffee. When he opened the cupboard he saw that the ashtray had been replaced in its customary position on the top shelf.

Ted went about filling the coffee maker on autopilot while he considered all of Juliette's behaviour during and since the call from Evie. She had to know more about what

145

had happened between Evie and Jakob, so why was she hiding it? He thought again about what Renton had said about a relationship between her and Jakob.

He carried their two cups into the lounge and put his on the coffee table. 'Juliette.' Ted didn't get a flicker from her eyes. 'Juliette.' He couldn't keep the impatience from his voice.

She responded to the louder utterance of her name, squinted at the drink he was holding and took it from him.

Ted sat on the couch next to her and she shifted more to her side. He picked up the remote and started flicking through the channels. 'I can't stop going over and over things in my head.'

She took a sip of her coffee.

'Trying to remember how Evie and Jakob were the last time we saw them.'

Juliette nodded but still seemed a little dazed.

'Maybe something major happened between now and last May we didn't know about.'

'Maybe.' Juliette curled herself against the arm of the couch.

Ted hated that he was laying a trap for Juliette but wanted to give her plenty of opportunity to come clean. 'Had Evie been in touch with you in between, you know, given you an inkling of anything that might be wrong?'

'Yeah. We spoke on the phone but that was about her treatment.'

Ted considered how to proceed. 'D'you think she wanted

to avoid seeing you because of the treatment? Is that why you didn't meet up before last night?' Had that been too obvious?

Juliette gulped coffee and hesitated. 'That was probably why. Are you going to settle on a channel?'

Ted was aware that he'd been robotically flicking through them and switched off the TV.

'You want to go to bed? I think I'd prefer to stay down here for a bit.'

Ted looked at her. 'Why didn't you tell me about Evie coming around here on Tuesday?'

She turned to him, her frown an immediate admission of guilt.

'I know she came here to talk to you about Jakob, but you didn't mention it to me or to the police. Not then, not now. Tell me what's going on.'

Chapter 34

Juliette's expression shifted from faux puzzlement to resignation. 'Georgie?'

Ted nodded.

She tightened her lips. 'I thought he was upstairs.'

'I think we should always assume he might be listening.'

'What did he tell you he heard?'

'You tell me.'

Juliette sat up straight and let the blanket fall to her lap. 'I'm sorry. I knew you had a lot on your plate at work.'

'It wasn't just an omission. We talked about the last time we'd seen Evie and Jakob on Friday night.'

'Evie wanted it to remain private, like Jakob did when he phoned you.' She raised an eyebrow.

That was fair enough, but Ted waited for her to continue.

'I also didn't want to worry you about Jakob.'

'What have you been hiding?'

Juliette took a sip of her coffee.

Ted wondered if she was playing for time.

'He'd tried to commit suicide before.' She put the cup down on the table.

That was the last thing he'd expected to hear. It was what made his death so hard to take: there was nothing in his character to suggest it was something he'd ever consider. Connor was the friend he'd been most anxious about, particularly after the comment he'd made when they last got together for a drink. But he'd shared those concerns with Juliette.

'That was why she came by.' Juliette cast the blanket aside.

'When did he do it?' Was all Ted could think to ask.

'Saturday before last. She wanted it to remain between the two of us and I respected her wishes.'

Exactly a fortnight ago. 'Jakob seemed absolutely fine before Evie's game.'

'I think that's been the problem. Jakob has spent the last year carrying on as if everything was normal, even during Evie's treatment. He was strong for her but when it was all over, he still wouldn't show any emotion. They were having problems before, but everything went on hold when Evie had her diagnosis. They went through hell together, but he gradually closed himself off from her.'

'How did he ...?'

'Pills and vodka. She got an ambulance out to him in time and they took him to the hospital and pumped his stomach.'

Ted shook his head. Why hadn't Jakob confided in him?

But they didn't have those sorts of conversations. He knew he missed his family, but like a lot of his male friends, emotions were taboo.

'He wouldn't talk to Evie about his attempt, carried on like it hadn't happened.'

'So why didn't you mention any of this to Renton?'

Juliette closed her eyes.

Ted waited while she breathed through her nose.

Eventually she opened her eyes again and seemed to have composed herself. 'Because I feel responsible. I wanted her to play her trust game. I thought it was her way of forgiving him for it.'

'But his suicide attempt wasn't a secret.'

'He'd done it in secret.'

'So you thought they could reconcile over after-dinner coffee?'

'It was a therapy exercise, not just some petty game.'

'You're right, it certainly wasn't.' Ted regretted the harshness in his tone.

Juliette clenched her jaw. 'He refused to talk to her, wouldn't go to anymore therapy sessions. I thought that if they were surrounded by their friends—'

'And you're sure the others don't know?'

'I told you,' she said firmly. 'It was between me and Evie.'

'Because they all seemed to be on your side when Renton was here.'

'That's because they all regret being part of it as much as I do.'

'And they've told you as much?'

'No, but it's obvious. Why don't you feel that way? Whether you were coerced or not, you played the game.'

'And because we did, Evie's dead? And now Jakob?'

Juliette's face froze and she nodded.

And for the first time since finding Evie and identifying Jakob's body, Ted felt the burn of tears.

Chapter 35

Ted was sure Juliette slept as fitfully as he did, but they both rose with Georgie the next morning for their traditional family breakfast. Sunday meant pancakes and Georgie started laying the table in readiness. 'Let's have it in front of the TV today,' Juliette suggested.

Ted knew why.

Georgie didn't need to be told twice.

They both sat before whatever cartoon Georgie wanted to watch and mechanically chewed their food until Ted's phone rang.

'Mr Middleton?'

Ted recognized Renton's dour voice. 'Any news?'

Juliette tensed as well and turned to him.

'I'm sorry to disturb you on a Sunday, but I was wondering if you both would mind coming down to the station.'

So here it was. But perhaps it was better that they come clean with him instead of having it hanging over them. 'Today?'

'If you can find time ...' Renton said, as if Ted had a choice.

Ted wondered if the others were about to get the same call. Juliette had already broken the news to them about Jakob's suicide. 'Can I ask what for?'

'There's something I'd like you to take a quick look at.'

That wasn't what they'd expected. 'OK. We have to quickly arrange a babysitter though.'

'I'm probably talking a few minutes. Why not bring your child along. Someone in the office can keep an eye.'

Great Oak Police Station was only ten minutes away and, when they'd parked up outside, Georgie was still in a mood because they'd dragged him away from the TV.

'Come on, scout. It's not every day you get to see inside a police station.'

Georgie was wrapped in a black scarf and bobble hat and reluctantly undid his belt and wriggled out of his seat.

They both took his hand and walked to the main entrance.

Did Renton have something else in store for them? Ted thought it unlikely that he'd allow Georgie to come along if he was going to interrogate them, but maybe he was luring them into a false sense of security. Ted told himself to stay calm. They weren't criminals. Even if Juliette had withheld some information, it had nothing to do with their presence at the crime scene. They'd been summoned there by Evie and had responded.

But neither of them said a word as they entered and approached the reception.

'We're here to see DI Renton.' Ted's throat felt dry.

The male desk sergeant looked like a teenager and had the corresponding acne. 'Um, I think he's on,' he checked his screen, 'second floor, walk past the canteen and you'll find him in the next office.'

They climbed two flights of stairs, and the smell of fried food hit them as they made their way along the corridor. They walked into an expansive open-plan office, with faded water-stained navy carpets. Renton was tucked behind a computer screen on the far side of the room, behind four rows of unoccupied desks.

'Thanks for coming in. And who's this?' Renton suddenly beamed at Georgie.

The genuine warmth in the detective's expression took Ted aback.

'There's a TV on in there.' Renton swivelled to the small glass-walled office behind him. 'And it's got a big comfy chair where my boss usually sits, and he needs a deputy. Can you mind his chair for him while I talk to your parents?'

Georgie nodded and Renton offered his hand. Georgie immediately took it and Renton led him in there, settled him in the swivel seat behind the desk and found the channel Georgie wanted.

Renton came out and shut the door behind him with a grin. 'I could drag you off in cuffs and he wouldn't notice.' The warmth had gone from his eyes.

The Dinner Party

Renton went to his desk, leaned down and closed whichever document he was working on. 'I'm waiting on the autopsy results for Mr and Mrs Eriksson but, in the meantime, I have some CCTV footage I'd like you to take a look at.' He gestured them to join him in front of the screen. 'Do either of you recognize this person?'

Chapter 36

Ted moved behind Renton's left shoulder and Juliette leaned in the other side.

On the screen a small window displayed a paused black-and-white clip. There was a blurry grey strip with a dark line in the top left of it. A time counter was frozen at the bottom.

'Here they are.' Renton hit the play button.

The clip was activated, the counter started, and Ted realized he was looking at a patch of driveway. The dark line was an elongated shadow that quickly advanced across the screen. 'Where is this?'

'The Eriksson's front drive.'

'I didn't know they had security cameras.' Juliette bent closer.

'Just at the front of the property.' Renton exhaled. 'Unfortunately.'

The shadow reached the bottom of the screen and its owner appeared behind it wearing a dark hooded coat.

'Looks like *they* might have known about the security.'

Renton observed. 'Any ideas?' He paused the clip so they could take in the figure.

They were quite slim but from the camera's angle it was difficult for Ted to get a sense of their height. 'Not immediately. Do we see their face?'

'Afraid not.'

Ted glanced over at Juliette.

She narrowed her eyes. 'That could be Evie or Jakob.'

'No. The camera recorded them both walking up the drive to the front door around one twenty. By the way, we spoke to their cab driver, Lithuanian fellah, Alex Simkus.'

'I know him.' He'd picked up Ted from the station on more than a few occasions. 'He's worked for Greenaway Cabs for a couple of years now. What did he say?'

'Said they hardly uttered a word to each other on the drive home.' Renton hit play again and the figure strode on.

Somebody else had been at the house? Ted looked at the counter at the bottom of the screen. 'At 4.12. That was after Evie called us.'

The figure disappeared out of sight under the camera.

Renton tapped his stubby finger against the screen. 'They get in through the front door, which means two things: either they had a key, or they were let in.'

'Evie might have thought it was us,' Juliette suggested.

'We wouldn't have got there that quick though,' Ted pointed out. 'Ibbotson's at least fifteen minutes from us.'

Juliette didn't respond but kept her attention on the screen.

'*If* Evie opened the door.' Renton sniffed. 'It might have been Jakob. You found Evie on the back lawn thirty-four minutes after this; at least that's when you said you needed the ambulance, and you said you think she'd been out there a while.'

'She was freezing cold,' Ted confirmed.

Renton dragged the slider at the bottom of the clip, pushed it forward to 4.36 and played it.

It showed Ted and Juliette arriving and tentatively walking up the driveway to the door.

After they pressed the doorbell and silently banged on the panel Ted watched himself step back and look up at the windows oblivious to the camera, his expression grave. Juliette called Evie and he left the message for Jakob. Soon after they both disappeared from sight as they headed around the side of the house.

'So, they're still there ...' Juliette said with dread.

Renton nodded. 'Nothing until this at 4.41.' He dragged the slider forward again.

They waited while the counter ticked over until they saw the hooded figure dash from the front door across the driveway.

Renton hit pause so the fleeing figure was suspended mid-step. 'Then there's nobody in or out until the patrol car arrives.'

'We were stood at the front door then,' Juliette recalled. 'We just missed them as they ran out. We thought it was Jakob.'

Ted scrutinized the hazy figure. 'We heard them upstairs. That's where they came from.'

Renton pushed his swivel chair back and rested his hands in his lap. 'And you've no idea why they'd be up there? After all, Mrs Eriksson is lying on the lawn at this point and according to your statement, there was nobody else upstairs.'

'The rooms were all empty.' Ted knew they'd checked.

'Because the rear of the house isn't covered by cameras, and there's no sign of Mr Eriksson on this footage after he entered the property at one twenty, we have to assume that he left via the gate in the back fence. That would appear to fit with the story he gave you about waking up in Nine Beeches, directly behind their home.'

Juliette straightened. 'Maybe they were robbing the place and we disturbed them.'

'Odd they'd walk up to the front door and either let themselves in or be admitted if they were a thief.' Renton wound the clip back to their first appearance and started playing it again. 'Look, their body language isn't remotely furtive. The hood is their only concession to that. From their pace it looks like they're in something of a hurry.'

'So you think they might have attacked Evie?'

'Or been some part of it. It's unlikely that somebody chose to rob the house at exactly the same time as Mr and Mrs Eriksson's domestic.' Renton indicated the screen. 'So, no clues. They're a stranger to you both?'

Ted squinted at the figure as it disappeared under the

picture again. Renton was right: it was impossible to work out if they'd been admitted or let themselves in. Who had they encountered when they first got inside?

'I don't know who that is,' Juliette said definitively.

Ted wasn't sure how she could have made such a declaration, because it really could have been anyone.

Chapter 37

When they got home Ted and Juliette settled Georgie in front of the TV in the back lounge.

'Do you need any other forms of pleasure, scout?'

Georgie had his blue plastic tray on his lap that contained a plate of chicken bites, a bowl of fruit segments, a tub of popcorn and a big glass of milk. He shook his head at Ted and smirked a little. He knew he was being spoilt.

It was good to see him smile again, and Ted closed the door quietly and walked out to join Juliette at the kitchen counter.

She opened the cupboard. 'You hungry yet?'

'We should eat something other than pancakes.'

'Crackers and cheese?'

'That'll be enough.' He watched her hunt them out. After their meeting with Renton they should both have been feeling at least a slight sense of relief. The detective's focus was clearly now aimed at the mysterious caller at Evie and Jakob's and not on the dinner party. But the footage threw up even more questions about what exactly had happened before and during their arrival at their friends' home. The recording exactly corroborated their statement, but Ted couldn't shake the image of the figure striding to the front door. Juliette had been very distracted during the drive home.

'How are you holding up?'

She turned from the cupboard and placed a new pack of crackers on the board. 'I just want our participation over for Georgie's sake.'

'I know but, even though we don't like him, we have to help Renton work this out.'

'And we will.' Juliette took a knife from the block.

'It's just you seemed quick to dismiss the person the camera picked up.'

Juliette cut the packet in half with the knife. 'I didn't dismiss them; I just didn't recognize them.'

'Nor did I, but it could have been anyone.'

Juliette turned her back to him to get the cheese. 'Exactly. Who would we know that would want to break into houses?'

'As Renton said, they could have had a key or been let in.'

She put the tub of cheese on the board. 'Or barged their way in when they opened the door.'

'But Renton was right. It looked like they were there on a mission.'

'Or an opportunist who was in the neighbourhood and saw them come home. Their house is all on its own.'

'So you're saying *they* might have attacked Evie?'

'Maybe,' Juliette replied eventually. She opened the tub.

Ted knew she had to be thinking the same thought. Was Jakob innocent? 'Jakob said he woke on the lawn next to Evie.'

Juliette dumped the lid and her shoulders tensed. 'So why did Jakob hang himself?'

'Because he believed he murdered her.'

'After he blacked out,' Juliette said dubiously.

'I told you, Jakob was acting like he was on something.'

'What are you saying? That the man in the clip force-fed him drugs?'

'No.' What *was* he saying? 'But it looks like a lot more went on between them getting home and us arriving there.'

'You're right but I don't think we should assume that Jakob is suddenly innocent. Maybe the guy was a friend helping him get rid of Evie.'

That had occurred to Ted. 'So where was Jakob when we arrived?'

'Well, he wasn't lying on the lawn when we looked out of the window,' she said sceptically. 'Maybe Jakob fled out of the back when we rang the bell. He might not have known Evie called us.'

'And what was the other person doing upstairs?'

'Hiding from us?' Juliette crossed her arms.

'Until we went to the station today, we thought there was nobody left who could tell us what happened. Now there is and they're still out there. Doesn't that make you uneasy? What if it's somebody we know?

'Somebody we know who disposes of bodies?'

'Don't act like that. There's clearly much more going on than we thought.'

'Then let's leave it to Renton.' Juliette looked down at the board. 'There's nothing more we can do, and I have to start thinking about my friend's funeral.'

'There'll be two funerals.'

Juliette concentrated on slicing the cheese. 'Don't forget you've got a call to make.'

Chapter 38

Ted reached into his back jeans pocket and took out the piece of paper with Jakob's sister's number on it. Renton had given it to him and asked him if he minded contacting her. She'd been into the station that morning and the detective said she knew nobody in the UK. But what would he say to her?

'Mrs Olsen?' All Jakob had told Ted about his sister was that she was quite a few years older than him and ran a recruiting business with her husband in Bergen.

'Yes?' Her reply was flat.

Ted thought he could hear a shower running in the background. He closed the door to the front lounge. Juliette was in the next room keeping Georgie company. 'I'm so sorry to bother you at a time like this but Detective Renton gave me your number and suggested I give you a ring. My name's Ted Middleton. I was a friend of your brother's.'

The water switched off. 'Yes?'

Ted was slightly at a loss for words. 'Uh ... is this a bad moment?' He flinched. What a crass thing to say.

'No. Just a minute, please.' Her tone remained strident.

Ted waited and the sound of the atmosphere changed as if she'd walked into a different room.

'Detective Renton said you were the last person to see my brother.' Her accent was softer than her manner.

Ted heard her sniff. It was the first indication she was grieving. 'Yes.' Ted wondered how much Renton had told her about the meeting in Roath Park. 'I'm so sorry for your loss.' He cringed again.

'It's difficult to ... accept what's happened.'

'We're all so shocked,' Ted continued when she didn't.

'I wanted to see him for myself.' She let the implications of that hang between them.

Ted imagined her in the mint green room where he'd been and the woman unzipping Jakob's purple face. He shuddered.

'Were you a close friend?'

Ted wasn't sure how to answer. He'd only seen Jakob twice in the last year. 'We lost touch for a while because of Evie's treatment. I've known him for about a decade though.'

'He never mentioned you.'

Did she sound suspicious? 'Friday was the first time I'd seen him in eight months.'

'And how was he?'

'Honestly, he seemed like his old self. Which is why we're still struggling to make sense of this.'

'You and your wife?'

'Yes.' It felt like an interrogation.

'Renton said you kept the meeting between my brother and yourself secret.'

'Jakob asked me to. Mrs Olsen—'

'Call me Brit.' But it didn't sound like the offer of someone who wanted to be friendly.

'I realize you're probably feeling very isolated.' Ted wondered why he suddenly wanted the conversation over. 'If there's anything I can do, you have my number.'

'Yes, I do,' Brit said, as if she fully intended to use it. 'What did Jakob say to you when you met him in the park?'

Ted wasn't expecting her to get into this now. But she obviously wanted answers as much as he did. 'He was acting very strangely, as if he was ...'

'Drugged. Detective Renton said.'

'Yes.' Ted guessed she was clearly a person who didn't need anything sugar-coated.

'Was he taking drugs?'

'Not that I knew of.'

'And never in the past?' There was incredulity in her voice.

Ted considered whether to lie. 'I remember smoking a joint with him a long time ago, but to be honest it wasn't really either of our thing ...'

'He caused trouble at home when he was younger,' Brit declared but didn't clarify the comment.

'Well ...' Ted didn't know any more about Jakob's family, 'from what I know Jakob was a good husband to Evie and conscientious at work.'

'It doesn't sound like you were *that* close,' she said dismissively.

'Evie was a friend of my wife's,' Ted started to explain.

'Don't take it personally. Jakob didn't let many people in. But he obviously valued your friendship enough to contact you instead of his family when he was in need.'

Ted couldn't detect any resentment. She was just stating the facts. 'I do know that Jakob was always trying to get the money together for a trip home, but that he and Evie struggled financially.'

'I've just driven past the house. It didn't look like they were struggling.'

The statement startled Ted. 'That was Evie's inheritance.' Why did he feel the need to explain? 'Her mother passed away and left them the family home.' It was clear Brit Olsen knew next to nothing about her brother's life in the UK.

'I think I have a lot of paperwork ahead,' Brit sighed.

Ted didn't know how to respond. He hadn't even speculated what would happen to the house. He knew Evie had no living relatives left, but had they made a will? After less than twenty-four hours in the UK – and having just seen Jakob's body – why was his sister worrying about paperwork?

'What did he say to you?'

Ted was momentarily thrown. 'In the park?'

'Yes.'

'That he didn't kill Evie.'

Silence.

'He said he couldn't remember what happened after they got home and that he woke on the lawn with Evie's body beside him.'

'So the detective said. And did you believe him?'

Ted paused. 'I've never seen Jakob raise a finger to Evie.'

'That's not what I asked.'

Ted took a breath.

She carried on. 'Nobody knows what goes on between married people. I love my husband, but he struck me in anger once. Gave me a black eye for a couple of weeks and it was clear to everyone I worked with what had happened.'

It was a very personal admission for someone he'd only been talking to for a matter of minutes.

'But it wasn't my fault and I wanted everyone to see it. When people asked me how I'd got the black eye, I didn't make any excuses for him: I told the truth. That shame was hard for my husband to bear and it never happened again. Everyone's capable of violence. I asked if you believed his story.'

Ted felt like he was about to betray his friend. But even though he doubted Jakob's version of events he recalled the figure in the security footage. 'Has Detective Renton told you about the other person who arrived at the house?'

She sighed as if disappointed to have her question answered with another. 'Yes. I've seen the clip.'

'I think we need to know who that is before any of us can draw any conclusions.' Ted heard two knocks.

'That's room service. I need to eat.'

It was a cold, functional announcement but Ted guessed that was how she approached everything. He was relieved though. 'I'm here all day, if you want me to call you back.'

'This is a little impersonal. I'd like to come over to talk to you face to face, if that would be OK?'

He registered she used the same phrase as her brother. 'Uh ... sure.' Suddenly it was the last thing he wanted. 'If you think that's necessary.'

'I have to get out of this hotel room. What are you doing later?'

'Today?' He just about kept the alarm from his voice. 'I'm having lunch with my family.'

'What time will you be finished?'

How could he say no? 'Probably after four.'

'Give me your address. I've got a hire car so I'll aim to make it over by then.'

Chapter 39

The doorbell rang at quarter to four.

Georgie turned from where he sat cross-legged in front of the TV to Ted and Juliette who were sitting on the couch. 'I'll go!'

'Hold fire.' Ted rose. 'It's for me.'

Juliette stood too. 'Stay here, we won't be long.'

She wanted to speak to Brit Olsen as well and Ted was glad of the support.

Georgie returned his attention to SpongeBob.

He knew they were keeping something from him, and Ted made a note to listen out for his presence in the hall while they talked. He closed the lounge's door behind them. 'I'll let her in,' Ted said.

Juliette went into the front lounge to wait.

When Ted opened the door, he was surprised to find a tall, slim man in a bottle green tracksuit standing outside. 'Alex?' Ted said.

It was the Lithuanian taxi driver from Greenaway Cabs, the one that had picked up Evie and Jakob.

Alex was in his mid-forties and had a thick mop of dark hair that was normally neatly gelled but today was in disarray. His bloodshot eyes and pained expression suggested he hadn't slept. 'Sorry to knock on your door on a Sunday, Mr Middleton.'

'That's OK.' He could see Alex's white Audi taxi parked at the gate. He'd been picked up in it several times, and Alex was a very chatty driver. He had two teenage boys and always asked after Georgie.

'I had a visit from the police last night.'

'So you heard about Mr and Mrs Eriksson?'

Alex bowed his head respectfully. 'They were your friends?'

'Yes. I think you might have driven them before.' With Jakob's habit of needing a last-minute cab after drinking too much wine, the chances were high.

Alex shook his head once. 'No. I'd not met either of them before.'

Ted registered how categorical Alex was. 'Is everything all right?'

'Yes,' Alex answered nervously. 'I just wondered if they'll need to speak to me again.'

'I've no idea. I think they're interviewing everyone,' Ted placated.

'Mr Copshaw wasn't very pleased with me.' Alex clasped his hands tight.

That was the guy who ran Greenaway. Now Ted realized why Alex was so agitated.

'He said he doesn't need police harassing drivers.'

'I understand.' Ted turned to find Juliette had arrived behind him.

'Hi Alex.'

Alex smiled broadly for her benefit but seemed to be even more flustered.

Ted addressed Juliette. 'Alex just wanted a private word.'

Juliette immediately picked up on the tension. 'Sure. Say hi to those boys.'

He grinned.

Juliette stepped away, but Ted guessed she was lingering behind the door.

Alex's smile evaporated. 'I've told the police all I know. Some of my family's documentation is ... not in order. Do you think they will come to the rank again?'

'I can't say for sure.'

'I had nothing to tell them. He asked me what they were talking about on the ride to Ibbotson, but I didn't hear anything.'

'In that case, I shouldn't think so.'

But Alex's forehead wrinkled further. 'I can't tell them anything more.'

'Then you don't have to worry. I'm sorry about all of this.'

'I'm just thinking of my family.'

'I understand, but if you've told the police everything you remember ...'

Alex nodded harshly. 'Yes. I have nothing more to say to them.' He checked himself for raising his voice. 'I'm sorry, I have come here bothering you when you're grieving.'

'Don't worry. I wish I could reassure you, but I get the impression Detective Renton has a much more solid lead.'

Alex frowned.

'Some security camera footage of another person going into their house.'

Alex's expression didn't shift.

'I'm sure they're trying to find them now. If they do call on you again, just give them the details of your other pickups that night.'

Alex considered that for a few moments. 'Yes. Thank you.' He nodded again. 'Sorry, I won't disturb you any longer.' He quickly turned and marched down the path to his car.

Ted closed the door. 'Poor guy ...'

But Juliette's face was impassive. 'He must have been worried sick to come knocking on the door.'

'He's just concerned for his livelihood.' But Ted could see Juliette wasn't convinced.

She looked briefly back to the closed lounge door. 'Could that have been Alex on the clip?' she whispered.

'Alex?' he scoffed but could see Juliette was serious. 'If Renton's spoken to him, he must be satisfied he's got nothing to do with it.'

'Maybe we should ask Renton when we speak to him next.'

'Alex wouldn't attack people there was a record of him taking home.'

'You don't know him.' Juliette kept her voice low.

'He's picked me up from the station a few times.'

'Exactly.'

'He's a family man, that's why he came here.'

'That's what he said to you anyway. We should definitely tell Renton about this.'

'But that'll guarantee Renton will want to speak to him again.'

Juliette bit her lip. 'Better he knows. If Alex is innocent, they'll soon be able to clear it up.'

Ted indicated Georgie, who had popped his head out of the lounge door.

'What's going on?'

'Back in front of the TV,' Ted said firmly. 'We'll be there now.'

Georgie obeyed.

Alex's car started up outside and he drove off at speed.

Maybe they *should* tell Renton. But Ted couldn't help acknowledging that Juliette hadn't been as conscientious about passing other information to the detective.

Chapter 40

Brit Olsen arrived dead on four o'clock and didn't speak when Ted opened the door. She was slender, a lot older than he expected, and looked nothing like Jakob. Her squinting eyes had tired lines around them that put her in her late forties. Her grey hair was styled into a layered pixie cut and dyed a subtle lilac colour. She wore a long tan raincoat and had a matching handbag over her shoulder.

'Come in.'

As she entered, he closed the door behind her and gestured to the front lounge where Juliette was seated.

She rose from the armchair in front of the mantelpiece to greet her. 'Mrs Olsen.'

'Call me Brit.' She extended her hand.

Juliette shook it. 'So sorry we're meeting under these circumstances.'

Brit looked analytically around the lounge.

'Can I get you a coffee?' Ted offered. His opportunity to shake her hand had obviously passed.

'Just had one.' Brit unfastened the top two buttons of her coat but didn't remove it.

'Please.' Juliette gestured her to sit on the leather couch.

She sat, back perfectly straight, and crossed her leg. She clasped her knee at the top of her patent brown leather boot.

Ted dropped into the second armchair and broke the awkward silence. 'How long are you staying in the UK?'

She seemed irked by the question and shrugged. 'As long as it takes.'

'Let us know if there's any way we can help.' Juliette settled back in her armchair.

Brit shifted her focus to Juliette and her features softened. 'That's very kind. I may well need to pick your brains for the funeral arrangements.'

It only struck Ted then how difficult a process that would be. Who would attend? With such a question mark over everything how many would want to pay their respects to Jakob?

'Maybe I could ask you to compile a list of people who *might* want to come.' Brit shook her head and opened her handbag. She took out a packet of tissues. 'Excuse me ...'

'That's quite all right.' Juliette assured her. 'It's been a horrible few days. We're all in a state.'

Brit gripped the packet of tissues tightly and the plastic crackled in her palm. 'Hard to know where to start; it was the last news I expected to receive.'

Ted noticed there were no tears yet. She retained her officious composure. 'We're all ... struggling with this.'

177

Brit swung her pale-blue eyes to him. 'So when you spoke to him, there was nothing he said that gave you the impression he was about to do something so drastic?'

'No, but he really wasn't himself. I tried to persuade him to give himself up but he—'

'Assaulted you.' Brit eyed his mouth.

Ted resisted sucking in his lip. 'It's not as bad as it looks. I was more surprised than hurt. It was so unlike Jakob.'

'Hmm,' Brit responded, as if she knew otherwise.

Juliette picked up on it. 'Has Jakob been aggressive in the past?'

'All siblings fight. I was lucky that I was much older than Jakob when we were growing up. He was a hyperactive child and sometimes my parents struggled to control him.' She took in their apprehensive expressions. 'But that was a long time ago.'

'How often was Jakob in touch with you?' Ted had to ask.

'He used to phone me fairly regularly. I have a very busy life though. Two teenagers and a job that leaves me little time to spend with them.' She cleared her throat. 'It's fair to say I lost touch with Jakob. I have to admit, he was always the one to make contact. But whenever he did, I knew I was getting the laundered version of everything.'

'Laundered?' Juliette repeated.

'I think Jakob, because of my achievements, felt he needed to compete. I don't know whether he felt inferior, but we could never have a real conversation about anything.'

Ted couldn't detect any conceit in the statement. It was her cold diagnosis of the facts.

'He would just go out of his way to assure me that everything in his world was perfect. Even when Evie was having her treatment, I couldn't draw him to talk about what they were really going through. When he found out that they couldn't have children because of him, he just dismissed it as he did all the other negatives in his life.'

Ted swapped a brief glance with Juliette. Neither of them had ever been told that. Evie and Jakob had refused to discuss their reasons for not having a family.

'He said he was going to come home to visit. That went on for a long time. I was just as much at fault though.'

'I certainly know how genuinely frustrated he was by that,' Ted felt compelled to say. 'He and Evie were always talking about it and then having to put it off another year.'

'I don't think their teaching jobs ever allowed them much leeway,' Juliette added.

Brit nodded. 'I offered him the money, last year, when Evie was ill. I suspected it was the wrong thing for me to do though. And I didn't do it graciously. I just became tired of having the same conversation. He was affronted, said he was capable of paying his own way.'

That was something else Jakob had never divulged to Ted. 'He turned it down?'

'No, he took it, but he never came to visit. Probably used it to pay for Evie's private treatment and that's completely understandable.' She sighed. 'But he probably saw it as a personal failure.'

Again Ted and Juliette made eye contact. Evie never had any private treatment.

'So when was the last time you spoke with Jakob?' Juliette asked.

'Two weeks ago. He contacted me when Evie went into remission and then he had gone quiet for a good few months. I thought it was because of the money. But he called me up all excited because he was going to surprise Evie by arranging to renew their vows.'

Ted and Juliette were speechless.

'He'd sounded genuinely happy, not the forced version I was used to. He said that after all they'd been through, he wanted them to have a fresh start.'

'So, two weeks ago?' Ted frowned.

'Yes.'

'Which day?'

'Saturday. In the evening.'

'Are you sure?'

Brit frowned back at his persistence. 'Positive.'

Hadn't Juliette told him that that was when Jakob had made his suicide attempt?

Chapter 41

'I didn't care about the money. I was just glad things were looking up for him. He'd been through a lot and I still feel guilty that I hadn't been more supportive. But it had been a taxing time for me. My eldest has been having some issues with drug dependence.' Brit swallowed hard. 'Something we're taking a day at a time.' She paused, briefly closed her eyes and inhaled. 'None of which you need to know.'

Ted recalled the story she'd readily told him about her husband giving her a black eye. 'I'm sorry to hear that.' It wasn't the first glib cliché he'd offered up to her.

'So ... as far as you were concerned, Jakob seemed happy when you spoke to him?' Juliette asked, mystified.

'We were probably talking for half an hour. I was going to the theatre, but I'm sure he would have chatted longer.'

It didn't sound like the actions of a man contemplating imminent suicide. Ted looked across at Juliette and her obvious confusion.

'Like I said to your husband though, Jakob never really

allowed people to get very close. I never met his wife, so maybe you have a better insight into their relationship. It was clear from his phone calls that he loved her, but it would be improper of me to attempt to defend him.'

Ted understood, particularly as Brit obviously had her own experience of domestic violence.

Brit continued. 'It's hard to accept that, after all they went through, it should end this way though. But maybe the trauma of her treatment had put undue pressure on them both. People deal with things in different ways and I'm sure Jakob would never have confronted his own feelings about it.'

She was right, but Ted still couldn't accept that Jakob had just gone crazy, no matter what had acted as a touch paper. His behaviour really hadn't been that much of a concern when he'd got in the cab after Evie's game. 'We're still hoping that Renton will find the person who called at the house.'

'Did you know many of Jakob's other friends?' Brit sniffed and put away the packet of tissues, her demeanour businesslike again.

'No,' Ted responded. 'He never spoke to me about them, although we did wonder if the figure in the clip was someone that Jakob or Evie might have called.'

Brit straightened again. 'Detective Renton has told me that they're going to access the records of both their phones. If either of them did summon them there, they'll have a number. What about his work colleagues?'

'I don't think either of them socialized with their fellow teachers,' Juliette replied. 'They had enough of the politics during school hours.'

'So they met at the school?'

Ted nodded. 'St Ballantine's. They both loved teaching the kids there.'

'What about Evie's friends?' Brit pressed.

Juliette answered. 'She was the same as Jakob. Had little social life outside of school. They preferred each other's company, but we'd get together for dinner once in a while.'

'You weren't close to Evie then?'

Juliette opened her mouth to answer but hesitated. 'Yes, I was, used to see her often. But she withdrew when she was having her treatment. Didn't want visitors, didn't want to see anyone, and I understood that.'

Brit turned that over for a few moments. 'But recently you only saw her at these dinner parties.'

'Yes.' Juliette didn't look at Ted. 'We'd talk a lot on the phone though,' she added.

'And she didn't give you any inkling that there was anything wrong with Jakob?'

Ted watched Juliette shift slightly in her chair.

'No.'

Why didn't she tell Brit about Jakob's suicide attempt?

'What about the other people at the dinner party?' Brit took out her hire car keys and fastened the catch on her handbag. 'Would they want to come to Jakob's funeral?'

Juliette stiffened. 'I don't know … I mean, I could find out.'

183

Brit held up her hand. 'Sorry, I don't want to put you in an awkward position. You have my number, so please let them know they can contact me.'

Juliette bit her lip. 'I will do.'

Brit fixed Ted with a stare. 'You're right. This unknown visitor is probably the only person who can tell us what went on. If that doesn't happen though, it may just be me at the funeral.'

There was an awkward silence, but Ted was reluctant to make a promise he might not keep. What if it was proved that Jakob did kill Evie? But it was looking less and less likely. Would he still go?

Brit stood and slung her handbag on her shoulder. 'I've taken up enough of your time.'

'Not at all.' But Juliette was on her feet.

'I'll keep you informed re the arrangements, but Detective Renton says he doesn't know how long the autopsy results will take.' Brit looked down at the coffee table and then realized her car keys were in her hand. 'Sorry, too much to juggle. I can see myself out.'

'Let me.' Ted walked to the front door with her and opened it.

Brit nodded once at him and left.

Chapter 42

'So ...' When Ted walked back into the front lounge, he assumed the word would be sufficient.

Juliette was seated in her armchair again. 'I don't understand. Evie definitely said he attempted suicide on that day.'

'Why didn't you tell Brit?'

'I didn't want to contradict her.'

'Brit or Evie?'

Juliette seemed lost in thought.

'It's unlikely Jakob would have had that sort of conversation with his sister just prior to taking a handful of pills.'

She shook her head. 'It's what Evie told me.'

'You're sure Evie said that Saturday?'

'I'm sure,' Juliette retorted loudly.

Ted closed the lounge door. 'OK, let's leave Georgie out of the conversation ...'

Juliette nodded apologetically. 'It doesn't make sense.'

'Which hospital was he taken to?'

'Why?'

'They'd have a record of him being admitted.'

Juliette narrowed her eyes. 'So we don't believe Evie now?'

'I didn't say that.'

'She didn't mention which hospital.'

'It's likely to have been Oakhurst General. What else did Evie say to you? Anything about them renewing their vows?'

'No.'

'What else did she say to you on Tuesday then?'

'Just … she just told me that Jakob had taken the pills. Maybe I've mixed it up. Perhaps it was earlier than that Saturday.'

Ted sat down in frustration. 'Well, you seemed sure a moment ago.'

'I was.' But now she wasn't.

'And even if it *had* happened earlier than that would Jakob have sounded so positive on the phone to his sister?'

'Maybe he wanted their last conversation with each other to be a good one. She just said he was never honest with her.'

'Not exactly.' Ted listened for Georgie in the hallway. 'Brit said he laundered his news. Besides, she told us he sounded genuinely happy.'

Juliette rubbed her eyes.

'How long did Evie stay?'

'Twenty minutes or so.'

'Did you know she was coming?'

'No. What's with the sudden interrogation?'

'I just wonder why she would turn up unannounced and urgently need to talk if it had happened much earlier.'

'She didn't urgently need to talk.'

'She was calm?'

'Yes. But as I hadn't seen her in such a long time I knew something was up. I asked her what was wrong, and she was reluctant to tell me.'

'That's understandable,' Ted conceded. 'But it must be difficult not to talk about an event like that.'

'Look, it's pointless speculating about what went on nearly two weeks before they came here for dinner.'

'Why?'

'Because neither of them can tell us now.' Juliette looked at the floor disconsolately.

Ted could see she was becoming upset again. 'I'm sorry. I want to be at Jakob's funeral and to do that I need to understand this.'

'But we'll never know.'

She was right. Evie could never explain exactly why she'd waited so long to speak privately to Juliette about Jakob's failed suicide attempt.

Chapter 43

Ted and Juliette spent the remainder of the evening sitting watching TV with Georgie in the back lounge, both immersed in their own thoughts, until it was time for the usual bedtime negotiations.

It took them both half an hour to coax their son upstairs. Was he thinking about his Auntie Evie and Uncle Jakob or just worried about confronting his fickle friends at school again? He wasn't even tempted by the prospect of a shower and Ted eventually had to be stern. He hated himself for raising his voice but knew the events of the weekend were taking their toll.

Ted waited outside the bathroom for Georgie to have a quick wash and brush his teeth. The door opened. Ted hadn't heard any sound of Georgie's electric toothbrush, but figured he'd scolded him enough. He followed him into the bedroom and Georgie slid under the duvet and lay with his back to Ted.

He sat on the bed. 'Try not to be angry, scout. We've all had a terrible weekend.'

'I know,' Georgie sighed.

'And don't worry about tomorrow.'

'I'm not. Not really. I'm more than capable of looking after myself.'

Ted smirked. Who had he heard saying that? He gently stroked the back of his head. 'See you bright and early.'

Georgie turned to him, perplexed. 'But you don't have to get up tomorrow.'

'True.' But Ted suspected the days off he'd been so looking forward to on Friday night wouldn't be that productive. Were they now effectively compassionate leave? He'd tried to persuade Juliette to have the start of the week off as well but understood why she wanted the distraction. He didn't want to be at home echoing around the dining room with only his thoughts for company. But he could save Juliette a trip to the childminder's, which meant she'd get an extra half an hour in bed for three mornings.

'*I* wouldn't get up if I didn't have to,' Georgie declared.

'That makes sense.' He pulled the duvet up to Georgie's chin. 'It'll soon be the weekend again though.' But he guessed, to Georgie, it may as well be a year away.

Georgie regarded him with concern. 'Are you going to be OK here on your own, Dad?'

Ted's throat tightened. 'Of course.'

'You won't be too sad about Auntie Evie and Uncle Jakob?'

'We're all upset, but that's OK.'

'Is it OK if I tell Jolian about what happened?'

'Why Jolian?'

'If he knows what happened, he might leave me alone, might even be nicer to me.'

Ted considered how to respond. 'Your friends should be nice to you, whatever's going on. Should always support you.'

'I know, but I don't have any friends like that.'

'You'll find them.'

'Do you have friends who do that?'

'Yes. I've got Auntie Orla and Uncle Connor, Auntie Kathryn and Uncle Rhys. That's why they came over yesterday. So don't worry about me, scout.' But Ted briefly recalled their expressions when he'd tried to persuade them to talk to Renton about Evie's game. 'Try not to care so much about what your friends think. Do your own thing.' That sounded like good advice to him. 'Let's keep what happened to Auntie Evie and Uncle Jakob to ourselves for now though.' How long would it remain a secret? Was it likely to be on the news the next day?

'OK,' Georgie agreed.

'And just tell those boys you're not interested in being in their gang.'

'But I am.'

'If they're not being nice to you, why would you?'

Georgie frowned as he turned that over.

'Just keep your options open, and make sure you brush your teeth first thing. I won't let that go again.'

Georgie looked shamefaced.

Ted kissed his forehead and turned off his lamp. 'Sleep now and don't worry. Your parents have always got your back. OK?' Ted heard the pillow rustle as Georgie nodded. 'Night.' Ted closed the door and headed down the stairs.

As he made his way along the hallway, he could hear Juliette on the phone to someone.

'Just take a few deep breaths,' she said. 'Ted's just finished putting Georgie to bed.'

He entered.

'Yes, Ted's OK, just emotionally exhausted like all of us.' Juliette looked up at him. 'Try to get some sleep. I really think tonight's fine to take a pill if you need to. OK, speak then.' She hung up.

'Who was that?'

'Kathryn.' She put the phone on the arm of the chair. 'I think it's just hit her. She's in a real state.'

Ted sat down next to her. 'Is she going into work?'

'Not by the sounds of it.'

'So why are you?'

'I need to,' she said definitively.

But Ted understood.

'How's Georgie?'

'I managed to turn off the lamp. I don't know if he's going to sleep though.'

Juliette got up off the couch, picked up Georgie's tray and plucked some stray popcorn off the cushions. 'I'm going as well, unless there's anything else you need to berate me for.' She didn't wait for a response but walked out into the kitchen.

Ted followed her.

Juliette put the tray on the counter and then reached for the light switch, pausing her hand there. 'Are you coming up?'

'Yes. Look, I didn't mean to grill you.'

'On which occasion?' She turned off the light and stepped past him.

He flicked off the lounge light. 'I just need to know what happened.'

Juliette started up the staircase but paused at the bottom. 'Everything's still raw. We've got us though. Let's not turn on each other. She strode up the stairs. 'I'll check on Georgie.'

Ted clicked off the hallway light and was left alone in the dark. He climbed after her, oblivious to the revelations the next day would bring.

Chapter 44

Ted and Juliette spent a fitful night, and both got up at six, an hour earlier than normal for a Monday morning. They silently drank their coffee in a trance-like state and waited for Georgie to come down at seven.

After breakfast Juliette paused at the front door, on her way to work. 'If you're not in the mood to do the decorating, don't bother,' she said before kissing him and heading down the path.

'And if you need to come home early ...'

She turned and smiled wanly. 'OK, I'll ring you later.'

Which meant she wouldn't be home until that evening, even though she already looked bleary-eyed and beat. He watched her open the gate and she glanced briefly back at him, before getting into her yellow Fiat 500 and driving off for the station.

Ted was glad to have the opportunity to drop his son off at school and turned to get a kiss before Georgie jumped out of the car. 'Remember, if your friends gang up on you, they're not your friends.'

'Is Peta picking me up from school?' Georgie changed the subject.

'No, I will. Maybe I'll take you for a Maccy D's.'

'Honestly, I'll be fine.' Georgie shut the door after him and scurried through the gates. He crossed the busy yard, joined the bottleneck of kids at the main entrance and disappeared inside.

Sitting in the car for a few moments, engine ticking over, Ted felt like normality had resumed too quickly. It was just over forty-eight hours ago that they'd found Evie. Less than that since Jakob had put a noose around his own neck.

He joined the line of drop-off traffic and was almost hit at the crossroads as he pulled out and failed to see a car coming from his left. He held up his hand in apology, but the young female driver beeped harshly and swore at him through her side window before accelerating away.

When was the last time he'd been as careless? He tried to focus on the road but withdrew into his thoughts again as he made the short trip back home.

When he closed the front door behind him the house seemed so silent. Slipping his keys into his pocket he hung up his jacket, rubbed the cold out of his hands and walked into the kitchen where there were still dregs in the coffee pot. He poured some and wandered over to the window overlooking the back yard. It looked as bleak as the sky above. He turned back into the room and his gaze settled on the table. He needed to fill the place with sound; however attempting to get Alexa to put music on for him didn't seem appropriate. He went into the front lounge, switched on the news and sipped his lukewarm coffee.

He wished he were in work, but now they'd cancelled Peta, the childminder, he would have to be around to pick Georgie up at 3.15. Ted pulled Juliette's TV blanket over himself and slid his body down the couch so that his head lay comfortably against the back cushion. He closed his eyes and quickly felt the weight of sleep on them.

But his mind kept turning over as it had in bed. Could he have done more to stop Jakob leaving the park? Why would Evie tell Juliette that Jakob had made an attempt on his own life if it wasn't true? Or had there been some other conversation about Jakob being an 'issue'? It was an odd way to describe somebody who was suicidal. Again he recalled Renton's innuendo about Juliette and Jakob. Paranoia? Or was the identity of the figure on the CCTV the only real question that needed to be answered?

Ted eventually fell into a shallow sleep, but his phone woke him, and he scrabbled it out of his back pocket.

'Mr Middleton?' It was Renton.

Ted could hear the detective's footfalls echoing down a corridor. He sat upright. 'Yes?'

Renton cut straight to the point. 'I've just had the autopsy reports back for Mr and Mrs Eriksson.'

Ted felt cold bubbles at the base of his neck and leaned his elbows on his knees.

'There were signs of strangulation, but Mrs Eriksson

died from head trauma after being struck by a blunt instrument, probably a garden ornament. We found blood on a small statue discarded by the hedge. Mr Eriksson: suicide by hanging and there was a significant amount of alcohol in his system. That we knew already.'

Ted suspected there was more to come.

'You told me no drugs were consumed at your little party.'

'No. There were no drugs,' Ted said firmly.

'We found considerable traces of Rohypnol. Difficult to detect, but after you told me what happened at the pavilion, I asked them to be thorough.'

'Rohypnol?' Ted stood.

'Do you know what that is?'

'Yes.'

'Not everybody does ...' Renton climbed some steps.

There was no point pleading ignorance. 'A date-rape drug.'

'Fast acting as well. Causes memory loss, anxiety, confusion, erratic behaviour. I'm really not sure what Mrs Eriksson would have gained from slipping it to him, so it was probably administered at your home.'

Ted knew he'd woken, that he wasn't having some bizarre dream. 'That's ... ludicrous.'

'I'm going to need to talk to you and all your guests again.'

Chapter 45

Ted hung up on Renton, selected Juliette's number but hesitated. He remained frozen like that for a few moments and then glanced at the time at the top of the screen: 8.57 a.m.

Juliette had told him she had a meeting from nine until eleven. He shouldn't phone her just as she was going into it. Call her afterwards.

He paused a couple of seconds more and then located another number.

'Ted?' Connor answered after six rings.

'Sorry, are you in the middle of something?'

'No, I'm working from home today. Didn't feel like going into the city. Are you OK?'

'How's Orla doing?' Ted recalled how fragile she'd looked as she'd left on Saturday.

'Not very well. She got up this morning to see the girls off to school but I told her to go back to bed. I'm worried about her. She hasn't slept, she's barely talking, and didn't eat a thing yesterday. She's just taken a pill and sparked out. I take it you're not decorating today?'

'No. I'm just rattling around here.'

'I'll ride the bike over. Just for ten minutes. If that's OK?'

Ted had been on the brink of telling him Renton's news but was relieved by his offer. 'Great. Now?'

'Yeah, I need to get out for a while. See you then.'

As Connor unzipped his blue biker jacket from his sinewy frame Ted could see he'd probably slept as much as Orla.

'I can't stay long. Where's Juliette?'

Ted hung it on a hook. 'She went to work.'

'Can't blame her.' Connor followed him to the kitchen counter.

'Coffee?' Ted had made a fresh pot.

'Please.' Connor strolled past the counter but halted halfway across the floor in front of the table. He turned around and came back.

'Renton called.'

Connor absently ran his hand through his tight black curls 'Any news about this other guy in the clip?'

'Juliette told you about that?'

'Kathryn told Orla.'

That figured. Juliette had been on the phone to her the previous night. 'No news on that but they found Rohypnol in Jakob's system.'

'What?' Connor's fingers paused in his hair. 'A roofie? Explains why he was acting the way you said.'

'But suicidal? Of all the people I know, Jakob was the last person I expected ...' Ted tailed off, realized he was saying it to exactly the wrong person.

Connor looked uncomfortable.

'Renton thinks it was given to him here.'

Connor turned over the implications. 'By one of us?'

Ted nodded and poured the coffee from the pot into two mugs. 'Either that or Evie gave it to him.'

'Why the hell would she do that?'

'Exactly.'

'She did use to dabble in a bit of recreational marijuana ... had a dealer.'

'Date-rape drugs though?' Ted handed Connor his coffee.

Connor shook his head and sipped loudly. 'You don't think it was part of her game?'

Ted doubted that. 'Why would it be?'

'It's more likely than one of us giving it to him. Have you told Kathryn and Rhys?'

'Not yet.'

'They're the most strait-laced couple I know. It couldn't be them.'

'I've not told Juliette either.' Ted realized it sounded like a confession.

Connor frowned. 'Why not?'

'She's in a meeting. I don't want this on her mind now.'

Connor put his mug down on the counter. 'Really?'

Ted knew it was an excuse.

'Think she's going to panic?'

Ted was relieved that Connor had acknowledged that. 'She feels guilty about playing the game.'

'Don't we all. It was a stupid thing to do, but perhaps we were just as stupid to keep it from the police.'

Ted was glad Connor was thinking the same. 'Renton wants to interview us all again.'

Connor's expression hardened. 'Then we do what we agreed.'

'But he's probably not going to be satisfied until one of us owns up to spiking Jakob.'

Chapter 46

Connor gazed contemplatively into his coffee. 'Did Jakob mention if they were going anywhere after dinner that night?'

'You mean he could have been spiked on the way home?'

'It's possible.' Connor glanced briefly over to the dining table. 'We don't really know what happened to them between one and four.'

'The police have their home security footage of them getting back soon after they left here. Plus the guy driving their cab, Alex, came to the house yesterday.'

Connor frowned. 'The Lithuanian guy? I know Alex. We use him as well.'

'He's already spoken to Renton,' Ted explained.

'Why did he come here?' Connor picked up his mug again.

'He's worried the police'll look into his family's documentation. Or lack of it.'

'Odd that he would call at your door though.'

'Said his boss was giving him a hard time because

Renton was sniffing around the cab office. Probably doesn't want anyone looking into his employment records. We had a visit from Jakob's sister soon after.'

'I didn't know he had a sister.'

'Much older, no-nonsense lady. He's been talking about going home to visit his family as long as I've known him.'

Connor lifted an eyebrow. 'I never got the impression Evie was keen.'

'Why not?'

'She always found an excuse.'

'It was a financial thing.'

Connor raised his hands. 'Look, you knew them better than me, but I think that one was going to run and run. I always felt Jakob wasn't that cut up about it either.'

'Jakob was desperate to visit.'

'Or was he happy for Evie to present him with a reason not to? If he needed to so much, he would have gone years ago.'

Ted wasn't so sure. 'His sister obviously had some problems with him when they were growing up. Sad that this was the thing that brought her over here.'

Connor nodded. 'So, earlier, when you said Jakob was the last friend you expected to top himself ...'

Ted knew he'd picked up on that. 'The last time we had a drink, just the two of us ...' He wasn't sure how to continue.

Connor waved his hand. 'I know, my head wasn't in a good place then. Things are different now though.'

'I was worried. Even discussed it with Juliette.'

Connor rolled his eyes. 'Don't worry yourself, or Juliette, about me.'

'So things are improving with you and Orla?'

Connor briefly grimaced. 'Improving probably isn't the best word. You and Juliette have never interfered though, and I'm grateful for that. Evie was the one who ...' He cut himself off.

'Her heart was always in the right place.'

'I know, that's why Orla and I put up with it. As if Evie and Jakob didn't have their own problems.'

Ted was curious. 'Did you have any idea what Orla wrote and put in her envelope?'

'Nope. And I'm certainly not going to tell her what I wrote.'

There was a brief silence between them.

Ted realized that Connor wasn't tempted to share. Was he? No, he barely entrusted it to himself.

'I'd better be getting off anyway. I don't want Orla to be alone when she wakes up.' Connor took a big slug of coffee. 'Let me know if you hear anything.'

'You should expect a call from Renton.'

Connor seemed lost in thought as he headed for the hall.

Chapter 47

As soon as he'd waved Connor off on his motorbike, Ted closed the front door and took out his phone to ring Juliette. He got her message so tried her office number.

'Environmental health,' a familiar female voice answered.

Ted recognized Juliette's colleague. 'Hi, Shawna, it's Ted.'

'Hey, Ted,' she said warmly. 'Haven't spoken to you in a while.'

'Is Juliette about?'

Shawna paused, as if offended by his reluctance to chat. 'She is but she's in a meeting at the moment. Shall I tell her you called?'

'Yes, please.'

'Emergency?'

'Not really. Can you just get her to ring me when she's done?' He felt guilty about not sharing Renton's revelation with her, but she was busy and now he'd left a message. He hung up and realized how abrupt he'd been. He had no time to worry about it now though. He dialled Kathryn and Rhys's number and his guilt intensified. When Juliette found out she'd know exactly what he'd done. Spoken to the others before her to make sure they were all going to be straight with Renton.

Nobody picked up. Didn't Juliette say Kathryn was staying home too? Ted cut the call and was about to try Rhys's number when somebody knocked on the front door.

He opened it and Zoe was standing on the step. She looked like she might be going out somewhere, as she had mascara applied to her eyelashes and wore a long red button-up coat.

'Hi, Ted.'

He immediately noticed the change in her usually stressed demeanour. 'Hi.' He was surprised to see her arms were empty, her hands in her pockets. 'No, Pip?'

'She's sleeping. She's been much better lately.'

So she wasn't going anywhere. She had subtle red lipstick on as well. Zoe was a pretty girl, mid-twenties and living in a house paid for by her wealthy ex-partner. They'd never met him, but Juliette had told Ted that Zoe was still recovering from postnatal depression. Outwardly she was always smiling and happy, but she had to be lonely. That was what had made Juliette enlist her to look after Georgie.

'I saw you come back in the car this morning. Everything OK?' Her brow wrinkled in concern.

'Yes, I'm off today anyway.'

'Juliette as well?'

'No, she had to go in.'

Zoe nodded, but it didn't appear to be a revelation. 'So you're on the school run?'

'I may as well be childminder today.' Was she after more babysitting hours? Did she need the money? Not from what Juliette had told him.

'Just a terrible business.' She shook her head.

'Yes.'

She bit the side of her red lip. 'Is there anything I can do?' Her blue eyes dipped.

You're a conceited idiot, he told himself. She was just being neighbourly. But why was she made up in that way? 'Thanks, but we're fine.' Juliette always invited her in, if only for ten minutes. He *had* to invite her in. But now he was getting a waft of her perfume and he'd never seen her look so glamorous. Maybe she would tell him why.

She didn't.

He hovered for a few seconds. 'I'm actually just on my way out,' he lied. But it was all he could think of to justify not admitting her.

Disappointment briefly registered on her face. 'Oh, sorry to hold you up.'

'No, it's fine, have to run a few errands.'

Her expression remained set, but something went out in her eyes. 'Just let me know if you need anything.'

'That's really kind, Zoe.' He grabbed his jacket from the hook for good measure.

Zoe still didn't leave.

He shut the front door behind him and slipped the jacket on.

She turned and walked with him down the path to the car. 'Have you heard anything from the police?'

Was she making conversation to cover up the awkwardness of the moment? 'We're just waiting to hear.' How much had Juliette told her? Irrespective, he didn't feel the need to get into a conversation with her.

They reached the end of the path and Ted scrabbled in his pocket and prayed the car keys were there. They were.

'I'll catch you later then.' She went through the gate before him and turned left to go into her own.

'OK.' Ted hung by the car and knew he'd have to get into it. He did so while Zoe walked up her path to the front door. It was going to look stupid if he didn't start the engine.

Zoe went through her blue door and shut it behind her.

What if she watched him through the window? It was ridiculous but he turned the Corsa over and pulled out. Where would he go? Georgie didn't need picking up from school for a good few hours yet. Ted accelerated to the end of the street and halted there.

Why hadn't he wanted to invite her in? He was sure Zoe wouldn't try anything as inappropriate as he was imagining. It had probably been completely innocent, but her manner had been so much different.

How long did he have to stay away before returning? Perhaps he would pick up some groceries. He was driving in that direction when he had another idea. Kathryn and Rhys were only five minutes away.

He turned right and made for the crossroads. He'd only been there once but he was sure he could remember the house if not the exact number.

But when Ted arrived in Dixon Street it was easy to identify their home, because Juliette's yellow Fiat 500 was parked in their drive.

Chapter 48

Ted squinted at the licence plate. It was definitely Juliette's, next to Rhys's red Lexus. He was about to pull into a space opposite the house but coasted to the end of the cul-de-sac and parked there. He switched off the engine but didn't get out. There could be no explanation for her presence. She'd told him she was in a meeting from nine until eleven that morning. He glanced at his watch: 9.49. She knew he wasn't a huge fan of Kathryn and Rhys, so wouldn't expect him to call here.

He took out his phone and rang her office again. 'Hi, Shawna? It's me again.'

'Oh … Ted.' She didn't sound as friendly this time.

'Sorry, I know Juliette's in a meeting, but I just wondered if there's going to be a break anytime soon so I can speak to her?'

'Um …' she paused. 'I don't think so. She's in the thick of it at the moment.'

'OK, that's all I needed to know.' Ted hung up.

He wondered what to do next. Juliette had obviously

set it all up before she left the office, if she'd ever been to the office. She'd been on the phone to Kathryn last night. Had this little meeting been planned then?

Ted started the car again. He would go home and wait for her to get in. Part of him hoped that would be soon, that she would tell him exactly why she'd stopped off here. But it was too premeditated, and he didn't want to see her sell the lie. He couldn't wait until then.

He switched off the engine and got out of the car. Closing and locking the door he walked to the house, passing the grass verges and trees that lined both sides of the street. The branches were bare, and the grubby silver sky made the surroundings even bleaker. He slowed as he reached the drive. What was he going to say? More importantly, what would Juliette say?

He didn't need to double-check it was her car as he strode up the slight incline of mossy tarmac. He paused outside the oak-veneer front door and considered that whatever happened next might change their relationship forever. He thought about their burnt secrets. Was Juliette the one with more to hide?

He listened at the panel but couldn't hear any voices. Was Rhys at home as well? Ted pressed the bulbous brass doorbell and stood back to wait. Nobody came to the door. Had Juliette gone somewhere with them?

He jabbed the bell again; leaning nearer to the wood and hearing it faintly ring inside. If there was anyone in, they knew he was here. Maybe he'd been spotted approaching the house and they weren't going to answer. Which was stupid because he'd seen Juliette's car in the driveway. He rapped the knocker hard.

Still no answer or movement.

Ted stepped over the flowerbed onto the lawn and peered past the curtain into the front lounge. Empty, except for two wine glasses and a bottle on the coffee table in front of the TV.

He crossed in front of the window and headed to the black-panelled side gate. Skirting two recycle bins, he pressed the clicker on the handle and pushed inside.

He was in the tight passageway between their house and the next. He closed the gate quietly behind him and trod silently along the path until he reached the lawn at the rear. Only a few days earlier he'd been doing the same at Evie and Jakob's.

When he reached the decking, he gazed up the length of their long lawn. The grass was unkempt and there was a dilapidated trampoline at the far end with a pool of water in its middle. The kids would be at school today. A pungent smell from the black compost bin against the hedge drifted into his nostrils.

Suddenly Ted felt like a trespasser. Had he missed something? But Juliette was deceiving him, and he had to find out why. Maybe Shawna had warned Juliette by now.

Ted advanced onto the decking and carefully peered around the first window into a long kitchen. There was a coffee mug on the breakfast bar, but other than that, the room was immaculate. No sign of anyone.

He crept past it until he was at the conservatory, which contained nothing but a hammock on a stand and a wooden crate of toys. Next to the frosted glass back door was a double window. Ted slunk to that and, keeping the rest of his body concealed by the wall, peered through the half-open plantation blinds.

For a few moments he couldn't see anything. There was no light on in the room. But as his eyes got accustomed to the gloom he could make out two people standing by the open door to the hallway. He cupped his hand around his eyebrows and tried to focus.

It was Juliette. She had her back to him, but he knew it was her. Standing in front of her was Kathryn. They were clearly in the middle of a heated argument. Kathryn wore an old grey tracksuit as washed out as her pallor.

He could just hear their voices through the triple glazing, but it was impossible to work out what they were saying. Juliette held her hands up and her head dipped as she castigated Kathryn.

Kathryn remained impassive before her expression grew hostile. She spat something back at Juliette and wiped her palm over her face in exasperation.

Then Kathryn's eyes locked onto Ted.

He could see her lips form his name.

Juliette turned to look at him.

Chapter 49

Juliette froze but said nothing, and Ted took a pace back from the window. He'd been spying, but Juliette was the one in the wrong. He remained where he was, and it seemed like a good few minutes before he heard a key turn in the back door. It opened inwards and Kathryn was standing there.

She frowned. 'What are you doing here, Ted?'

But he wasn't going to allow her to put him on the back foot. 'I rang the doorbell and knocked loud enough.'

'Sorry, we were in the middle of something.'

'So I gather.' Ted waited for her to elaborate but she just stood back.

Ted entered the kitchen via the conservatory.

'Go through to the lounge.' Kathryn sealed the door.

Ted felt uneasy as he walked into the room on his left. Juliette stood there, panic in her eyes. 'I just spoke to Shawna. She said you were in the thick of it.'

Juliette remained rigid. 'I'm sorry.'

'Why all the lies?' Ted's face felt hot.

'It's my fault.' Kathryn had followed him in.

Ted kept his gaze on Juliette.

'I asked her to come,' Kathryn continued.

Ted turned to her. 'Why? And where's Rhys?'

'Upstairs,' Kathryn answered. 'He's locked himself in the bedroom.'

'What the hell for?' Ted returned his attention to Juliette. Her face was blank.

'Juliette, what's been going on?'

She still didn't answer.

A thump from overhead.

Juliette's eyes rolled briefly to the ceiling.

'Shall I go and ask him myself?'

'You're probably the last person he wants to see.'

When he fixed Kathryn again, she stood in front of the doorway to prevent him from passing. 'Why?'

'We should tell him the truth,' Juliette interjected.

Ted knew that this was no longer about Juliette wanting to hush up their involvement in Evie's trust game.

'You're welcome to go up and see him ... if you want your neck broken.' But Kathryn remained blocking the doorway.

'Why wouldn't Rhys want to see me, Kathryn?'

'I knew we'd get the call from the police; have to explain why we didn't go to the house.'

Ted realized what Kathryn was talking about. 'Evie and Jakob's?'

Kathryn sighed. 'Evie called us too, early that morning. Asked me to go over there. I wanted to but Rhys wouldn't let me. Told me to let them sort it out between themselves. I know I should have gone. I said call me again if it gets out of hand, but it already had.'

'Why didn't you tell us?'

'I could have done something, but I didn't. I got a call late yesterday afternoon. Renton had accessed Evie's and Jakob's phone records and found the call to us. Wants to interview us this morning at eleven.'

'Why not be honest and just say you thought the argument would fizzle out?' Ted swivelled back to Juliette. 'So is *this* the truth?'

Juliette nodded once but was still tongue-tied.

'I panicked. Asked Juliette to come here, Ted.'

It still didn't make any sense to him. 'And why is Rhys so angry with me?'

Juliette bit her lip and looked over his shoulder at Kathryn.

'That's my fault too,' Kathryn said firmly.

But Ted wanted to hear it from Juliette. 'What aren't you telling me?' He took three steps towards Juliette and she recoiled as if he was going to strike her.

'What's wrong with you?' But then Ted realized she was reacting to something behind him.

'Rhys, no!' Kathryn yelled.

Ted heard something crunch against the back of his head but was unconscious before he struck the carpet.

Chapter 50

Ted felt something solid against the back of his head and when he lifted it the pain surged in. He opened his eyes to darkness. Had he gone blind? There was a strong aroma of polish in his nostrils. Where the hell was he?

As his senses returned, he realized he was lying on his back. He tried to rise but struck a solid edge with his eyebrows. Was he inside a box? His breathing accelerated and he shot his hands out in front of him, but they didn't encounter any lid or barrier. But when he dropped them to his sides, they landed on something soft and cold. He gripped the object to his right, ran his fingers along its smooth contours. It was a leather shoe.

Ted groped above him and found the edge he'd bumped into. He took hold of it and used it to push his body forward and lever himself up to a sitting position. He felt dizzy as the blood drained from his face and the wound on the back of his head pounded under tight skin. He touched it and flinched.

He recalled the event that had preceded his waking up

there. Where was Juliette? Ted waited for the wooziness to subside as his eyes became accustomed to the dark. To his right was a thin strip of light that seemed to be coming under the bottom of a door. Scrambling first to his knees and then shakily to his feet something metallic hanging over him butted his scalp as he straightened but he ignored the pain.

He pushed on the door in front of him, but it was solid in the frame. His hand scrabbled down its smooth surface to the handle. He leaned against it, pulled on it. He was locked in.

Voices, low and in another room somewhere.

Ted held his breath and then put both his palms against the panel in front of him as he strained to listen. Why had he been confined like this? If he'd been attacked surely Juliette would have got him to a hospital. He attempted to hear the muted conversation, but the jangling circulation in his ears drowned the words.

Should he stay silent? But what if Juliette was in danger? He reached into his back pocket for his phone, but it was empty. There was no way of knowing exactly how long he'd been unconscious.

Ted banged on the door twice with his fist. 'Open this door.' His throat was dry and struggled to get the words out. He waited.

The voices continued.

'Open this door, now!' He found enough volume the second time.

The voices stopped.

They'd heard, whoever they were. Ted kept upright by holding onto the door and waited.

Footsteps approaching.

Ted rapped again. 'Get me out of here. Now!' he demanded. But he felt on the verge of blacking out.

A loud impact from the other side made him jump backwards from the panel.

'Rhys!' Kathryn's voice.

'Kathryn?' Ted staggered back a little and fell against a soft wall behind him. Coats?

'Just go! Cool off!' she yelled.

Footsteps and then a front door slammed.

Ted lifted himself off the coats. 'Kathryn?'

'Yes. We're unlocking the door. Are you calm?'

'When wasn't I calm?' he answered and felt his legs wobble beneath him.

A key turned in a lock and suddenly daylight flooded into his cell. He squinted against it and took in the two figures standing in the hallway before him. Juliette and Kathryn.

Juliette came forward and put her hand under his right elbow. 'It's safe to come out now. We had to lock you in there for your protection. I'd better call an ambulance.'

'No, I'm OK.' Ted didn't know for sure but his need to find out what was going on overrode everything else. He glanced down and realized he'd been lying in Kathryn and Rhys's understairs cupboard, his head under the bottom step, shoes everywhere. He bent to pass through the doorway and cool air hit his warm face.

Kathryn trotted to the window overlooking the drive and peered through. 'He's gone, left on foot. Better get Ted out of here before he comes back.'

Ted freed himself from Juliette's grip. 'What the hell is happening? What did Rhys hit me with? A baseball bat?'

'His fist.' Juliette's eyes shifted to where Kathryn was.

'I'm sorry, Ted.' Kathryn walked back to them. 'It *is* all my fault.'

'You already said that. Why did Rhys attack me?'

'I was scared it would come out when Renton interviewed us. When we told him about the game we played for Evie.'

Ted looked at Juliette. She was wearing a resigned expression.

'What I wrote down. What Rhys burnt.'

Ted could still feel the wound fizzing as the room spun.

'Come and sit down.' Juliette was supporting him again.

Kathryn wiped stray strands of hair from her forehead. 'I'm sorry, Ted, but I told Rhys we'd slept together.'

Chapter 51

Ted frowned and even that action tugged at the lump on the back of his head. 'Why would you tell him that?'

'Come on.' Juliette guided him into the lounge.

Ted allowed her to lead him there and was grateful to drop down onto the green leather couch. As she examined him, he closed his eyes and waited for the room to come to a standstill.

'I think he's got concussion.' Juliette sat next to him. 'Call an ambulance.'

Ted opened his eyes and touched her hand. 'No, just give me a moment.' He blinked a few times, but the walls were still shifting.

'Ted ...'

'Wait,' he said firmly.

'I'll grab my first aid.' Kathryn was about to head out of the door.

Ted held up his palm. 'I'm fine. Just tell me what this is about.'

'Get the kit,' Juliette ordered sternly.

Kathryn disappeared to fetch it.

'I'm sorry.' Juliette kissed his hand gently and released it. 'I should have told you. When you arrived we were in the middle of it: Kathryn had just told Rhys about her affair.'

'With me?' Ted hissed as he tried to rest his head against the couch. 'How come I don't know about it then?'

'I'm sorry.'

'You've apologized already.'

Kathryn was back. She handed a plastic white zip-up bag to Juliette and then seated herself in the green leather armchair opposite him. 'This is on me. I've been seeing somebody else.' She clenched one hand in the other. 'For nearly two years.'

That was a shock to Ted. Kathryn and Rhys always seemed so together. Even when they'd been writing down their secrets, he hadn't suspected either was capable of infidelity.

'I used to go out with Rhys's brother, long before we were married. Then I met Rhys. But when my father died Rhys's brother was a real comfort to me. And things ... reverted to how they'd been.'

Juliette produced some antiseptic from the bag and a piece of cotton wool.

'Rhys and his brother have a long history. They've always fought. If I told Rhys who I'd really been seeing he would kill him. I mean actually kill him.'

'So you told him it was me?' Ted retorted incredulously.

'I told him it was somebody he knew, so he kept pushing me. I chickened out. Knew what he would do to his brother if

I told him the truth. So I lied and said you. Rhys respects you.'

Ted snorted. 'Not anymore.' Before Juliette could apply it, Ted took the antiseptic-soaked cotton wool and lightly touched it to the back of his head. He sucked in air to stem the pain and then examined the swab. No blood, but it felt like there should have been. 'You could have made something up when Renton questioned you. Nobody else knows what was in your envelope.'

'Rhys had been getting increasingly suspicious. I'd been careless. It was a matter of time before he confronted me.'

Ted tried to recall the exchanges between Kathryn and Rhys the night they'd played the game.

'It was a stupid thing to do but when Rhys has simmered down, I'll tell him the truth.'

'That's what we should all be doing,' Ted said flatly.

Juliette took the swab from him and tipped some more antiseptic on it. 'So if Renton wants to know what all of us wrote you will too?'

Ted had walked into that. But he had to respond. 'If it can explain what happened to Evie and Jakob ...'

Kathryn picked up on the atmosphere between them and was silent.

'I really think you should let a doctor examine you.' Juliette handed him back the cotton wool.

'I'm OK.' But the burn seemed more intense when he dabbed it again.

'Rhys isn't usually violent.'

Ted looked askance at Kathryn. '"Usually"?'

She rose. 'You'd probably better finish doing that at home though. Our interview with Renton starts soon.'

Juliette nodded. 'Are you OK to stand?'

Ted got to his feet but still felt punch-drunk. He regarded Kathryn. 'Will *you* be OK?'

'I think so.' Kathryn glanced at her watch.

'Are you going to wait for Rhys to come back?' Ted asked.

'No time. He needs a few hours anyway.'

'Have you got the keys to his car?' Juliette put the kit on the coffee table.

'No. I think he's got them with him.' Kathryn nervously tugged at her sleeves.

'Let us drop you there then,' Ted offered.

'Would you?'

Ted felt better that they weren't leaving her alone. He was badly shaken by Rhys's attack, but more by the notion that he was capable of it. 'So what are you going to say to Renton?'

Kathryn took her house keys from a dish on the coffee table. 'I'll answer all his questions, but I'm not going to tell him anything he doesn't need to know.' She took his phone from the mantelpiece and handed it to him. 'Sorry, I didn't want you calling the police when Rhys tried to boot the cupboard door in.'

'There was no reasoning with him.' Juliette swallowed.

'Can you phone Rhys? Maybe I should.' He located his number.

Kathryn exhaled. 'You could try.'

Ted called it and a ringtone started in another room.

Chapter 52

Juliette and Kathryn were silent as the three of them left the house together. Kathryn pulled the front door closed as Ted scanned the street. No sign of Rhys.

'Shall we go in your car?'

Juliette was right. Her 500 was going to be tight for three of them. Ted pointed. 'It's parked down there.'

Juliette aimed her key at her yellow Fiat, and it beeped twice as she locked it.

But Ted hesitated. 'Will it be safe on the drive?'

Kathryn hooded her eyes. 'He's angry with me not Juliette. And he's not a vandal.'

'Not just angry with you,' Ted reminded her.

'I'll talk to him.' Her expression was grim. 'When I get back, I'll straighten it out.'

Sounded to Ted like she was dreading that conversation more than the interview with Renton. He unlocked his car and slid into the driver's seat. Juliette got in the front and Kathryn slumped in the back. They said nothing as he reversed and turned.

Ted accelerated along the street and paused at the cross-roads. Still no sign of Rhys. The sooner Kathryn spoke to him the better. He didn't like the idea that he was nursing a completely unjustified resentment. Ted understood why Kathryn was reluctant to tell Rhys who she'd been seeing but why choose him? It didn't seem plausible, but maybe Ted *was* the first name she thought of. He glanced at Kathryn in the mirror and she stared right through him. 'Kathryn.'

She didn't respond.

'Kathryn, are you OK?'

She nodded weakly.

He turned to Juliette. She swivelled her head to her friend.

'Would you like me to wait at the station with you?' Ted offered Kathryn. 'What time do the girls come home?'

Kathryn didn't answer.

'Kathryn?' Juliette prompted. 'Do you need to pick the girls up?'

She snapped out of her trance and her eyes darted as she thought about it. 'The minder brings them home at half four. I hope I'm back by then.'

'And that Rhys has calmed down.' Ted was angry that he'd been dragged into this situation. 'Are you all right?'

Juliette eventually realized he was talking to her. 'Just shaken.'

'I can drop you at the house if you don't want to wait at the station. Then I can go back, pick Kathryn up and take her home.'

'No, I'll wait and come back with you both,' Juliette insisted.

'Failing that, we could involve the police.' He studied Kathryn's reaction in the mirror.

'No,' she said determinedly. 'I need to work this out with Rhys.'

They drove on for a few moments, Ted examining the pedestrians but not spying Rhys.

'Why did you come to Kathryn's?' Juliette asked.

Was he going to mention the visit from Zoe? That was why he'd got into the car. But when he thought of it his behaviour seemed ridiculous. He would tell Juliette about it but not now, not in front of Kathryn. 'I had a call from Renton,' he deflected. 'He said there was Rohypnol, the date-rape drug, in Jakob's system.'

The two women silently absorbed this.

'I told Connor and he came round.' He had to quickly explain. 'I tried to call you at the office to tell you, but Shawna said ... well, you know.' He felt a pang of guilt. That wasn't strictly the order of things.

Juliette was deep in thought.

'Rohypnol?' Kathryn repeated. 'How could he have taken that?'

'Or been given it.' Ted watched her in the mirror.

Kathryn shook her head.

He kept watching her.

Chapter 53

Kathryn got out of the car at the police station just before eleven.

'We'll wait for you here,' Ted said as the cold wind blew in.

She nodded and closed the door. Wrapping her dark teal cashmere shawl tighter around herself she set off unsteadily towards the main entrance, her normally neatly coiled hair rippling around her pale face.

'So how much of that did you know before you went over this morning?'

Juliette wound down the window. 'I need some air.'

Ted waited.

'I didn't know about her affair until today. She called me last night and said she wanted to see me because Renton wanted to interview her about the phone call Evie made to her that morning.'

'And didn't tell me.'

'Kathryn knows how you feel about keeping stuff from the police. She didn't want a hard time.'

Ted wasn't sure Kathryn was so easily intimidated by him, but another thought occurred to him. 'Don't you think it's strange that Evie called Kathryn?'

Juliette opened her mouth to reply but her eyes darted. 'Evie and Kathryn aren't that close. Were we called first?'

'I ... assumed so.' Juliette bit her lip.

'But you told Evie we were on our way. Why would she then call Kathryn as well?'

Juliette blinked as she followed Ted's train of thought.

'Kathryn said Evie phoned her and that Rhys told her not to get involved. Was it only after that call that Evie rang us for help?'

Juliette didn't have an answer.

'I suppose they're five minutes closer. Isn't it weird that Kathryn wouldn't help Evie though? And why didn't she mention it earlier? At least to us?'

They both watched Kathryn climb the steps to the station and disappear through the entrance.

Ted wondered exactly how much she would tell the detective about the dinner party. 'Because she didn't tell him upfront will Renton now think she's hiding something about the drugs in Jakob's system?'

Juliette inhaled slowly. 'All I know is Kathryn was worried about what would come out when Renton interviewed them. Rhys already had suspicions about her affair and had been sniping at her since the trust game. She cracked and told him about it this morning and he'd already gone off on her when I arrived. He'd locked himself upstairs.

Didn't want to see her and she was pleading with him through the door.'

'You should have left.'

'I wanted to, but then Kathryn said she'd told Rhys she'd had the affair with you. Besides, I couldn't not help her.'

Kathryn didn't help Evie when she needed it. But Ted kept that thought to himself. He undid his seatbelt. 'So what happened after Rhys hit me?'

Juliette shivered but didn't wind the window up. 'You collapsed and that stopped him in his tracks. Kathryn got him into the room next door, but he wouldn't listen to reason – he wouldn't believe she'd lied about having the affair with you. I was ringing the police, but she begged me not to. Took your phone and asked me to lock you in the understairs cupboard while she calmed him down. You were still semi-conscious.' A tear rolled down her cheek. 'I wanted to call an ambulance, but you said no and got to your feet.'

Ted struggled to recall any moment between the blow and waking in the cupboard.

'You were really dizzy, losing consciousness. I guided you to the cupboard; you sat on the floor and then slid down the wall. Rhys started yelling at Kathryn again. I locked the door so he couldn't harm you. Then I went to the kitchen to tell them I was going to phone for an ambulance. That was when Rhys started kicking the door.'

Ted knew the rest.

'But you still haven't said why you called at the house.'

'Zoe came around.' Ted realized it was going to sound foolish.

Juliette frowned. 'What for?'

'Just being neighbourly, I suppose. It was unusual though. She was wearing make-up.'

That took a few seconds to register with Juliette. 'Make-up?'

'Maybe I was being stupid, but it's just I've never seen her like it.'

'She *is* applying for jobs. Perhaps she had an interview.'

That made sense. 'She did say Pip was sleeping though, so I don't think she was going anywhere.'

Juliette twigged. 'You mean you there on your own and her a lonely single mother ...'

'It just seemed a little odd.'

'Her sister sometimes babysits for her.' But Juliette didn't appear completely convinced.

'She gave me the impression she wanted to be invited in ...'

'She always wants to be invited in.'

'I know and I think I probably completely misread it,' he added quickly. 'I just wasn't in the mood to talk, so I gave her an excuse. Said I was going out. So I did.'

Juliette wound up the window again. 'So you spoke to Connor about the Rohypnol and then you were going to tell Kathryn and Rhys? Before you spoke to me?'

'I tried to call you. Shawna told me you were in a meeting.' It was a convenient excuse but not entirely the truth.

'I needed to talk about it. I just can't get my head around how Jakob ended up with that stuff in his bloodstream.'

Juliette shook her head. 'This just gets worse and worse.'

Ted had to ask. 'Was Evie still ... dabbling?'

'I don't think she's done anything like that for years.' Juliette seemed very certain.

'That you know of. I wonder what it was that Jakob took when he had his overdose? If he really did try to commit suicide.'

'Why would she lie to me about that?'

Ted delicately touched the wound at the back of his head. 'I don't know. Evie's the only one with any drug connections, but without her testimony, Renton's going to be looking to us for answers.'

Chapter 54

'What about Evie's dealer?'

Juliette frowned at Ted. 'She didn't have a dealer.'

'She used to. Her ex. What was his name?' Ted racked his brains.

Juliette shrugged.

'You know, Guy something. Grant, that's it. What was his surname? You must remember her ex.'

'That was a long time ago.'

'We must have photos of him. Grant Tulley. That's it.'

'Do we really have to drag up that part of her past?'

Ted was casting his mind back to the New Year's Eve that Evie had got them the joints. 'Perhaps it isn't in the past though.'

'I'd know.'

'When she was diagnosed, she went off the radar.'

'I respected her privacy.'

'But she clearly kept stuff from you.'

Juliette filled her chest. 'Even if she did have a dealer, why would she drug her own husband with Rohypnol?'

'I can't see Kathryn or Rhys having any reason for doing it – they were busy with their own issues anyway. When Evie wanted to play the game, it was news to all of us, correct?'

'Yes.'

'She hadn't mentioned it to you beforehand?'

'You know that,' Juliette said firmly.

'There was nothing else Evie mentioned to you? Something she wanted Jakob to admit?'

'Aside from his suicide attempt?'

'Something else she'd want to coax out of him?'

'No. She was distraught about the attempt. I told you.' Juliette's tone hardened further.

Juliette was right. What possible reason could Evie have had for giving Jakob a date-rape drug? Rohypnol made you forget. It wasn't a truth serum.

'I wonder if Renton has a record of any other calls being made that night.' Juliette zipped her collar tighter.

'To the person in the CCTV clip?'

She nodded. 'Maybe this is all irrelevant. If Renton has a record of that call, then they're the one who can explain what happened at the house.'

'Unlikely though, particularly if he still needs to talk to Kathryn.' But Ted was puzzled as to why Evie had called her. How much more of her life had Evie concealed or lied about to Juliette? 'We should tell Renton about the suicide attempt. He can find out from the hospital if it really happened.'

233

Chapter 55

While they waited for Kathryn, Juliette said she needed to catch up with some emails and focused on her phone, but Ted was getting increasingly concerned about her. She just seemed to stare at the screen. 'Are you sure you're all right?'

She nodded and tapped the display for his benefit.

Ted had no desire to go to the hospital to be examined, but knew it was something she normally would have badgered him about. They'd just been through a traumatic episode at Kathryn's but had Juliette told him everything?

He accessed his own work emails but couldn't concentrate. Instead he opened Facebook and put a name into a search.

Grant Tulley

There were only five in the results and he studied the profile photos of each. The third was a man in his thirties with a shaven head and a little girl on his lap. But when he looked closer, despite the extra pounds, he was sure it was Evie's ex. Ted had been at a couple of parties Grant had attended in the early days of knowing Juliette. He was the sort of guy who had seemed cool to have around when they were in their twenties – always buying rounds of shots and getting them cheap tickets for gigs from the booking website he ran. But despite his party-supply sideline, Evie had grown bored of him as a boyfriend. It had all been amicable, however, and she still scored the odd joint from him. Jakob hadn't really liked him being around and that was understandable. He'd properly disappeared from the scene when Evie and Jakob had got married.

Ted tapped his photo and confirmed it was definitely him. His profile said he was single. He was still living locally in Brayford, a satellite village four or so miles away.

Ted sent a friend request and held his breath, as if he would get an immediate response. But when he scrolled through Grant's posts, he could see the last one was the profile photo, which he'd updated in 2018. Only three other profile pic updates preceded it, Grant's features getting progressively slimmer as far back as 2012. Not exactly a social media animal. He did have over four hundred friends though. If he was still dealing maybe he used Messenger to communicate with his clients.

Ted closed the page and wondered if Grant would remember him.

Juliette's phone rang and he glanced across at her display. *Kathryn*

Juliette raised her eyebrows at him and answered. 'What's happening?' She sat up straighter in her seat.

Ted couldn't hear what Kathryn was saying.

'Don't worry, we really don't mind waiting, however long it takes.' She listened then swallowed. 'I'm sure he'll call you soon. Just take a deep breath. And ring me as soon as you're done. We'll come and pick you up ... Yes, stay with us tonight. Just keep calm. OK.' She hung up.

'What's happening?'

'Renton wants to question her for longer.'

'What for?'

'She doesn't know what else she can tell him, but he's adamant. She said she's arranged for her brother to pick up the kids and they're going to stay at his house, so we can go home.'

Ted looked at his watch. Just after midday. She'd been in there for over an hour. 'She hasn't heard from Rhys?'

'No. And I don't want her going home alone.'

'Maybe Renton doesn't believe her story.'

'About Evie calling?'

'Yes. It still seems strange that she kept that conversation from us. I'd be suspicious. Maybe he thinks that's her in the clip.'

'That's ridiculous.'

'I suppose he only has her word for it. That figure couldn't be Rhys, he's too hefty, but it could be Kathryn.' As Ted thought it out loud, he could see why she was being detained.

'But she was in bed with Rhys. He'll confirm that ...' Juliette trailed off.

'Perhaps Renton will be speaking to him next. If they can find him.'

'Why do you say it like that?'

'Well, it's not going to help, is it? He's Kathryn's alibi and he's gone AWOL.'

'He'll be back,' Juliette insisted. 'And then they can clear this up.'

'She didn't mention that Renton wants to see Rhys?'

Juliette looked thoughtfully at her phone for a moment. 'No.'

'Seems odd. Maybe Renton thinks Rhys will lie for her anyway.'

'So, you really think that Kathryn's in the clip?' Juliette asked incredulously.

'I don't know. Don't you think it's possible?'

She pulled on her safety belt. 'Let's go. We'll wait at home.'

'Juliette, don't you think it's possible?'

'Maybe Renton's asking her all about the game and what she put in her envelope. Perhaps that's what we'll all have to tell him now.' Juliette clicked the belt into place.

'Perhaps.' But he suspected she'd said it to silence him. He pulled on his own belt and started the engine.

A few minutes after they'd pulled out of the police station and had slowed at some lights, Juliette's phone rang again.

'Connor?'

Ted briefly looked over at her.

'No, I'm in town with Ted. Slow down.'

Ted checked the road as the traffic surged through the lights and then tried to read Juliette's expression.

It changed to alarm and she sat forward. 'What?'

Ted had to quickly apply the brakes to prevent them going into the back of the car in front.

'Yes, we're only ten minutes away. We'll be straight there. Connor? Connor?' He'd cut the call. She immediately hit redial. 'Connor's at Gallcott Parkway. Orla's on the rail bridge threatening to jump.'

'What?' But Ted knew he hadn't misheard.

'He wants me there now. Needs me to talk her down.'

Chapter 56

Ted pulled them off the busy main road and sped them to the train station via the back streets. Juliette rang Connor's number again.

'Anything?'

'Going to voicemail.' But she kept trying.

'What about phoning Orla?'

'If she's on the brink of jumping, I daren't. Watch out!'

Ted returned his attention to the road in time to swerve around a group of kids in hoodies. They hurled abuse as the Corsa shot past.

He jerked the wheel and took a sharp right back onto the main road. The station was only one set of traffic lights away now, but they were red. Ted decelerated as they reached the back of the waiting cars.

'Come on!' Juliette yelled.

Seconds ticked away.

She put her hand to the door. 'I could get out here. Go the rest of the way on foot.'

'They'll change now.' But Ted counted past twenty as they remained frozen.

'I'm getting out.'

'Wait! It's not going to be any quicker!' Ted willed them to change.

Another nine seconds later, they did, and the traffic rolled painstakingly forward. Ted dodged around the car in front and cut across to the station entrance.

Juliette already had her door open. 'See you in there.'

The parking was at the rear, but Ted wasn't about to let her go alone. 'I'm coming as well.' He left the motor running and opened his door.

Juliette crossed the small ticket office area and when Ted reached her she'd accosted the young guard at the barrier.

'Let me through! And alert the police. Somebody's about to jump off the bridge!'

He regarded her impassively but didn't budge.

'Open it!'

Juliette's command spurred him into action, and he used his pass to open the turnstile.

'Call the police!' Ted barked as he followed her through.

They emerged onto the platform and Ted looked left to the metal bridge that allowed passengers to cross over to the opposite one. He jogged towards it. A cluster of people filed over it and he squinted at their faces. But they were all moving. Nobody static.

'There!' Juliette was running in the other direction and stabbing her finger.

At the opposite end of the platform, about a hundred yards away, was a second metal bridge and Ted could see the top half of two figures standing on it. He started to sprint.

The people who were standing and seated on benches glanced up from their phones. Ted checked the arrivals display.

Next train to arrive at this platform: 12.10 to Shearbourne. Due.

And at that moment a female voice over the speaker announced its imminent arrival.

Juliette kicked off her heels and ran.

Nobody had an inkling of what was about to happen.

'Call the police!' he shouted at the bemused faces he passed. 'Somebody's going to jump! Stop the train!'

A teenage girl frowned and pulled out an earphone.

It was too late, even if they alerted the driver. It would be approaching the station at speed.

Juliette pumped her arms and Ted gained on her. It was definitely Orla and Connor on the bridge. Orla was crouching and as he got closer, he could see she was lying on her front along the edge of the low metal wall. Connor stood about four feet from her.

A metallic swish on the rails to his left. The train was close. Ted could hear the low boom as it got nearer. Should he call to them? Would that alarm Orla and provoke the wrong reaction?

Juliette was nearly at the foot of the metal steps when he caught up with her.

'Let me go up first,' she told him breathlessly and didn't wait for his response. She started climbing in her stock-inged feet. He went up after her.

When they reached the top, Connor held his hands out to them, his expression rigid.

Juliette halted. 'Orla!'

Beyond Juliette, Ted could see her face. There was no panic there, not even any acknowledgement of their presence. She had one leg a few feet off the floor of the bridge, the other along the top of the metal wall.

'Orla come down. I'm here now.'

Orla shook her head at Juliette, her eyes unblinking through her fringe.

Juliette took a pace forward and Orla arched her back, thrusting her leg over the drop below her.

Connor held out his palm at Juliette. 'Nobody's coming any closer. Just talk to Juliette, Orla. Tell her why you're doing this.'

Juliette slightly retreated.

Ted looked briefly right. The track bent around a ravine. No sign of the train but a rumble said it was about to appear.

'Orla, nothing can be as bad as this.' Juliette's voice trembled. 'Put your foot back on the floor.'

Orla shook her head again sluggishly.

Ted wondered if she was on medication. Connor had said she'd swallowed some sleeping pills, but maybe she'd taken something stronger.

'Nobody's going to do anything. Please just put your foot back on the floor before you lose your balance,' Juliette pleaded.

Orla stuck her foot out further over the drop and her body teetered.

Ted fought the reflex to run forward. He and Connor were too far away to grab her if she fell, but he knew he couldn't afford to get any closer.

'If you won't talk to me, listen to your friend.' Connor bent his legs, as if in readiness to lunge forward.

'Let's you and I go and have a talk.' Juliette held out one hand. 'Come on.'

Ted could see something register in Orla's eyes.

'Just the two of us. There's nothing we can't sort out.' Juliette didn't move but kept her fingers outstretched.

Orla pulled her leg in from over the drop.

Juliette nodded encouragement. 'That's it, come back. We're not leaving without you.'

Orla's knuckles whitened as she repositioned herself on the edge of the wall.

'We all love you. This isn't the answer.'

Orla blinked rapidly, as if she'd just woken up there.

Out of his eye, Ted saw the train dart in their direction. It was slowing down to stop, its speed still deadly. Connor met his eye and then whipped his attention back to Orla.

She'd squeezed her eyes shut.

'Orla!' Juliette screamed.

Connor dived at Orla as she let herself roll off the edge.

He caught her as she lost contact with her metal perch and, for a brief second, he held her there. But her weight was too much and as he tried to get a purchase around her waist he toppled over with her.

Ted reached them just as they both plummeted out of sight.

Only Connor cried out.

The train roared by.

Chapter 57

Ted felt the draught from the train and the vibrations in his chest. They remained suspended in their positions while the black roof of the locomotive zipped by. Its hiss seemed to suck every other sound out of the moment. Ted's fingers gripped the cold metal where Orla had been. Part of him didn't want the train to stop moving below because he knew that, when it did, they'd have to confront what had happened to their friends.

But as the rear of the last carriage resounded and severed the brief, warm vacuum, reality quickly settled on them. Ted could hear people's voices on the platform and then a woman screamed. Juliette stood a few feet behind him, frozen, her hands still helplessly raised. Her mouth was open, her eyes unblinking.

There was nothing to say. Ted spun back to the wall, something at his core trying to prevent him from looking over.

More commotion from the platform.

He stared down at the ground below, but there was nobody on the tracks.

'What can you see?' Juliette's choked voice asked from behind him.

The train had to have taken them both further into the station. He lifted his eyes, following the tracks to where the rear of the train was slowing. About twenty yards behind it was a shape. It wasn't big enough to be a body, but he guessed it had to be Orla or Connor. His eyes refocused on something smaller lying on the side of the track a few feet before it.

'All passengers on platform 1 please return to the main concourse. The train doors will not be opening. All passengers on platform 1 please return to the main concourse.'

Ted barely heard the announcement. Was one of them still alive? Still caught up under the train?

'Ted, what can you see?' Juliette was closer now.

Then his eyes detected a movement to the far right of the tracks, only about a hundred feet from where he was standing. It was Connor, lying on his side, his one arm jerking. 'It's Connor.' He pointed for Juliette's benefit. 'There!'

Juliette clutched his shoulder and looked over it. 'What about Orla?'

As he hurried back to the top of the bridge steps, he heard Juliette react to what was further up the tracks.

'All passengers on platform 1 please return to the main concourse. The train doors will not be opening. All passengers on platform 1 please return to the main concourse.'

His heels resounded on the steel steps as he thudded

quickly down them. Ted stood on the edge of the platform and for a moment couldn't see Connor. Then he spotted the blue of his leather biker jacket protruding above the furthermost raised track. Ted dropped down onto the dirty grey gravel.

'Ted, don't!' Juliette shouted behind him.

Ted looked right. No train entering the station. He had to get to Connor.

'Get out of there! You'll be electrocuted!'

Ted briefly froze. She was right: the tracks were live.

'Get back on the platform!' a male voice yelled.

But Ted only hesitated for a few seconds before stepping forward, jumping between the wooden slats until he'd reached Connor.

Connor was in a worse state than he'd thought. Even though it appeared the velocity of the train had spun him clear, he'd sustained a serious injury to the left side of his head. Dark blood matted his hair and pooled in the chippings under his face. Then Ted saw the state of the arm as its spasms continued. It had been yanked out of its socket, the blue sleeve the only thing keeping it in place. 'Connor ...' He reached out a hand but withdrew it. Had to wait for a paramedic. 'Connor, can you hear me?'

'Ted!'

He looked over to where Juliette was crouching at the edge of the platform with three men next to her. One, wearing a high-vis vest, was restraining her in case she tried to follow him. A fourth was climbing down onto the track.

'Get an ambulance, I think he's still alive!' But Ted couldn't be sure. His arm movement was decreasing. 'Connor?'

He opened both his eyes, his left lid fluttering against the sticky blood. His lips unstuck and he painfully drew breath. His pupils darted, as if he were trying to recall what had happened.

'Connor, it's Ted. You're safe. Don't move, don't try to say anything. The ambulance is on its way.'

'Orla?' Connor frowned and a red rivulet trickled over the side of his nose.

'Don't talk, just hold on. They'll be here in no time.' Ted looked back at the bridge. They *were* safe, tucked away at the side of the tracks. But sitting there he realized how far Connor had been thrown.

'Is she OK?' Connor's eyes fixed him intently and he shifted his shoulder to get up but gasped in agony.

'Don't move, OK? Just wait for the paramedic.' What else could he say?

Chapter 58

Ted only registered the scalding heat of the taste-less coffee as it reached his stomach. Juliette sat opposite him in the hospital waiting room. He recalled climbing up into the ambulance with her but had very little memory of the journey to Oakhurst General. The pain from the injury at the back of his head had with-drawn, like it had been sapped by the intensity of what had just happened.

How long had they been waiting there? He concentrated hard on the face of his watch: 2.33. Through the low hiss in his ears he realized Juliette was speaking.

She was on the phone and nodded at him as she responded to whoever was on the other end. He peered into the empty paper cup in his hand and gently squeezed against its waxed shape.

'That was Kathryn.' Juliette was suddenly sat on the chair to his right.

'You told her?'

'Yes. And Renton still hasn't finished with her.'

Ted tried to focus. That situation seemed like a week ago. 'He'll be here sooner or later. What about Georgie?'

'I told you, Peta's going to drop him home and Zoe will be there to look after him.'

'That's right.' Now he remembered the conversation. He tried to absorb his surroundings. How long ago had they given their statement to the policeman who had accompanied them? He was nowhere to be seen. The waiting room was a lot quieter than when they'd arrived; only a handful of people were now sitting in the rows of grey chairs in front of them.

'Are you sure you're OK?' Juliette put her hand against the nape of his neck.

The warmth of her light touch seemed to spread over his shoulders.

'Maybe you should speak to somebody.'

'We both should. But let's see how Connor is doing first.' A female doctor had told them that he was the only one to survive. Ted assumed the platform was closed while they recovered the remains of Orla's body. He still couldn't shift the expression that had been on her face before she'd dropped out of sight. Through whatever drugs she'd taken she'd acknowledged their presence and still gone ahead.

'I thought Orla was so much stronger than Connor ...'

Ted had believed the same. 'Could it have been the medication she was taking?'

'Maybe. Did Connor talk about it this morning?'

This morning? He couldn't believe what had transpired since then. 'Only that she'd taken some pills to help her sleep.'

'What else did he talk about?'

Ted racked his brains. 'The Rohypnol, we discussed that. He didn't stay long. Said he wanted to get back to her so she wouldn't wake alone.'

Ted's attention was drawn to a surgeon in green scrubs who entered the waiting room area and scanned the people assembled there. But they recognized someone in the second row and gestured. A couple stood and followed him through the swing doors.

Ted's thoughts drifted back to the bridge, him coming down the steps and then jumping onto the tracks. 'I kissed Shawna.' He anticipated Juliette's hand breaking contact.

Her palm remained there.

'At the summer party last year, in the Fire Station bar,' he continued.

Juliette hesitated before replying. 'Don't do this now.'

'That's what I wrote on my piece of paper, what you forgave me for in front of the others.'

'Ted, this isn't the time.'

He couldn't look at her. 'You never came.'

'Georgie was ill,' she said emotionlessly.

'You called me after I'd got there.'

'I told you to stay. Pointless both of us missing it.'

Ted felt like his words were coming unbidden. 'Georgie was ill, and I was at the party.'

'It was a stomach upset, nothing serious. I told you he was fine.'

She was being too reasonable. Him doing it while she was at Georgie's bedside was what made him sick with guilt. The drunken kiss had been nothing but that. Too many glasses of wine and their lips held together for a matter of seconds. But she'd offered to wait with him for his taxi to arrive and he'd known why.

It had been a warm night and her mouth had been hot against his. A few seconds and he'd broken away from her. He'd told her to go back to the party and she'd pouted. Shawna was only in her mid-twenties. He'd met her a few times at Juliette's office, conceded she was gorgeous, but that had been the night he'd discovered her friendliness towards him masked something else. It hadn't been premeditated on his part. He hadn't even wanted to go to the party. But as Juliette wasn't there Shawna had taken it upon herself to introduce him to everyone. She'd hardly left his side. He hadn't eaten and he'd drunk too fast.

All pathetic excuses. And even though their kiss wouldn't have aroused suspicion in anyone watching, he'd been complicit. While Juliette had been nursing Georgie. And that was what he would always regret. 'After what happened today—'

'Don't.' Juliette's hand still hadn't lifted away.

'There was nothing there. But for a few seconds ... I just want to be honest.'

'Just stop. I knew about it,' Juliette stated simply.

Ted met her eye for the first time since the confession. 'How could I not? I know who Shawna is. She told me she'd looked after you, made sure I knew as soon as I got into work the next day. Made it sound so harmless. I guessed she was covering herself.' She shrugged.

But Ted didn't believe the gesture. 'I'm sorry.'

'That's OK.' She enunciated the 'OK' and fidgeted with her phone. 'I've already forgiven you for it.'

'It was just a stupid party game.'

'Then why write it down?'

'It was all I could think of.' And that was the truth.

Juliette's fingers slid away from his back. 'You could have scribbled anything.'

She was right. Despite his reservations about playing he'd been an opportunist.

'I think we can survive your secret.' She turned away from him.

'Mr Middleton?'

Ted noticed that a diminutive, balding middle-aged man in green scrubs was standing in front of them.

'Mr Lowney is out of danger now. His arm was broken in three places and he's lost a lot of blood but he's in a stable condition.'

He felt at least one knot loosen. 'Thank you.'

'His lack of serious trauma leads us to believe that he probably rolled across the top of the train.'

'Is he conscious?' Juliette asked.

'Yes. But barely, we've administered morphine for the pain.'

Juliette took Ted's hand and squeezed.

Ted put his over hers but was immediately considering the reality that Connor had woken to.

'He's asked to see you.'

Ted frowned. 'So soon?' What would they say to him?

'Normally we wouldn't allow it, but he says it's of some urgency. If you'd just like to follow me.' The surgeon headed for the ICU.

Ted looked at Juliette and they both stood.

The surgeon swivelled back to them. 'Just Mr Middleton, he was specific.'

Ted frowned again, but Juliette released his hand and nodded.

'Go on, quickly,' she said.

Ted followed the surgeon into the recovery area.

Chapter 59

Ted struggled to keep up as he was led past several curtained-off sections of the ward. The surgeon slowed as he reached a set of blue drapes and gestured for him to make his way behind them.

'He knows about his wife?' Ted couldn't be the bearer of that news.

'He's just been informed, so he's still in shock. Please take that into consideration. Two minutes only.'

Ted stepped past him and entered the area. A masked nurse was making clipboard notes on the other side. She nodded and vacated the tight space.

Connor was lying in the bed on his back, his bandaged head raised and his pulverized arm in traction. He had an oxygen mask over his face and was connected to a drip. He wasn't asleep or unconscious though. His eyelids were squeezed shut in pain.

Ted stood there for a few seconds before he spoke. 'Connor.'

He immediately opened them, and they were blurred and full of anger.

He took a pace closer to the bed. 'Looks like you had a lucky escape.' Ted regretted the words before he'd finished uttering them.

Connor breathed faster and the oxygen mask blurred around his nose.

'Whatever it is you're feeling ...' Ted felt his own eyes burning. 'However helpless you're feeling, we're right here. All that's important now, before anything else, is you recovering.'

Connor croaked something, but it was incoherent. He lifted his good hand with the cannula in the back of it and tried to remove the mask.

'I don't think you should do that.'

But Connor dragged it off and took a gulp of fresh air. His complexion was pale and shiny with sweat.

'Just take it easy.' He wondered if he should summon a nurse.

'I don't know what she was taking ...' Connor slurred. But he didn't appear to have the strength to speak.

Ted guessed the morphine had kicked in. 'You don't have to do this now.'

'When I got back from your place ...' he inhaled and flinched, 'she'd got out of bed.' He let his head fall back on the pillow as if the exertion were too much.

Ted waited.

'I told her about the Rohypnol. She went quiet. She dressed and said she needed some fresh air. Wanted to go for a walk. She still seemed strung out on whatever pills she'd taken. I offered to go with her, but she said no.'

Connor closed his eyes for a moment. When he opened them again, he regarded Ted as if he was surprised to still find him there. 'I knew something was wrong. I followed her. She walked through town, wandered aimlessly round. Then she went to the station.' Tears rolled down both his cheeks. 'I saw her standing on the bridge and I realized what she was doing there.'

'We all tried to stop her.' Ted knew it was no comfort.

Connor's head lolled forward, but he fought the drowsiness. 'Orla got up on the wall and wouldn't come down. I thought Juliette could talk some sense into her. Orla just kept saying sorry.'

'Why?'

'She wasn't making much sense, said it was her fault. That she should never have tried to get even.'

'With who?'

Connor shook his head. 'I had her ...' He was back in that moment, the panic suddenly vivid in his eyes. 'I was holding her. She wriggled free.'

'I think you should leave now.' A nurse was at Ted's shoulder.

Connor looked through Ted, as if staring at the drop below the bridge. 'She didn't want me to save her.'

'That's enough.' The young nurse went to Connor and tried to fit the mask back over his mouth.

Connor's eyes remained open.

'He should rest now. The doctor will let you know when you can see him again.'

But Ted loitered at the curtain.

'Can you go back to the waiting room, please?' the nurse said sharply.

Connor blinked heavily and then he was out again.

Ted returned to Juliette, who stood as soon as she saw him.

'How is he?' She lowered her voice, so the other people couldn't overhear. 'Did he speak to you?'

'He's pretty sedated. But he said that Orla was apologizing to him on the bridge. Saying she shouldn't have tried to get even.'

Juliette sat again. 'Did he know what she was talking about?'

'No. Sounded like she was doped up on her strong sleeping pills.' Ted seated himself and scanned the waiting room. 'Where's the police officer gone?'

'He was taking a call the other side of reception the last time I saw him. Maybe he's speaking to Renton.'

'I'd better let him know when he comes back.'

Juliette quickly stood again. 'I need to go to the bathroom.'

'Are you OK?' Ted thought Juliette looked as white as Connor had.

'I'll be fine.' But she headed off immediately.

Ted watched her go. He decided to give her a few minutes and then see if she was all right. His phone buzzed in his pocket, so he took it out and looked at the display.

Grant Tulley has accepted your friend request.

Chapter 60

Juliette got out of Ted's Corsa in front of Kathryn and Rhys's house in Dixon Street. It was just before five in the afternoon and already dark.

'If he approaches you, just get in your car.' Ted looked beyond her to her Fiat 500 and Rhys's red Lexus on the drive. There were no lights on in the windows of the property. Maybe Rhys hadn't returned.

The policeman at the hospital had said that Renton wanted to interview Ted first about the incident at the railway station at six o'clock and that Kathryn was still with him. It was six hours since they'd dropped her off. Why was he holding her so long? With Connor heavily sedated they'd decided to pick up Juliette's car so that she could go home and relieve Zoe while Ted went to the police station.

Juliette edged cautiously up the drive to her yellow car and it beeped twice as she unlocked it.

If Rhys came out, they'd have to tell him what had happened to Orla. But Ted hoped they could avoid any confrontation with him until Kathryn had set him straight.

He kept an eye on the front door as Juliette slid into her car, but nobody appeared. Even though he was beginning to believe she might have already forgiven him for Shawna, Ted wondered if she would ever reveal her secret.

She closed her door, started the engine and reversed down the drive.

At the end of the road, they both turned in different directions, Juliette towards home and him back to town and another conversation with Renton. But Ted had over an hour before he was due in the detective's office and as he waved and accelerated away from Juliette, he again felt guilty about where he was headed in the meantime.

Ted had passed The Mason Arms in Brayford every day on the train for the past seven years, but he'd never been inside the place. Brayford was a nondescript village with only a tyre centre, a new estate that dwarfed the original houses and the pub.

He parked up on the street outside and walked through the entrance. The gloomy interior told him it was one of those dives you marvelled at still being open. There were a few guys in work-clothes laughing noisily at the bar, but the remainder of its considerable floor space was full of empty tables with dog-eared menus on them. Looked like Grant Tulley hadn't arrived yet. The barman eyed him warily, so he ordered a Coke and sat in the corner furthest from the others.

When he contacted Tulley via Messenger from the hospital waiting room, he'd got an instant response. He opened his phone and re-examined it.

Hey, Ted! Remember you from Cactus Jake days. Longtime no see. Help you?

Cactus Jake's was their old haunt, a Mexican restaurant and late-night bar. Grant had always been very generous with the shots, but Ted had quickly realized he was buttering them all up as clients. Was he still dealing? From his message it sounded like he might be. Ted had suggested a quick drink in The Mason Arms and knew that couldn't have been more convenient for Tulley.

Ten minutes later a very tanned Tulley came in with a pasty girl young enough to be his daughter. He was carrying even more extra pounds and wearing less hair than his most recent Facebook profile pic. Despite the weather, he sported a short-sleeved orange polo shirt, faded jeans and flip-flops. He raised a hand at Ted and then made a drink gesture.

Ted shook his head and waited while Tulley got a pint of lager for himself and a Red Bull for his companion, before telling her that he'd be back soon. He crossed the floor of the pub and extended his hand.

Ted got up and squeezed it. Tulley's fingers were cold. 'Good to see you.' Tulley looked like an overinflated version of the handsome surfer guy he used to be and there was definitely more salt than pepper in the shaved hair on his head.

'You're a blast from the past.' Tulley seated himself on the chair opposite.

Ted sat. 'How long's it been?' But he knew exactly.

'How's the old crew?' Tulley beamed.

Tulley had never been part of the group. When he realized Evie had moved on, they rarely saw him. When they did, he was always with different people he never introduced them to.

'You're still with Juliette?'

'Yes,' Ted replied, slightly surprised. Maybe his memory wasn't as addled as he expected.

'Thought you guys were for keeps.' His smile remained but he knew reminiscing wasn't the purpose of the visit. 'You're lucky to catch me. Just back from PortAventura.'

'All right for some.' Ted knew the niceties wouldn't sustain long.

'So, what can I do for you?' Tulley tried to look mystified.

'I'm having a bash for Juliette. A big one. Wanted to get the old gang back together.'

He nodded. 'Sounds good.'

'Obviously, you're on the guest list as well as some other old faces.'

'None as well-worn as mine,' Tulley joked.

Ted forced a brief chuckle. 'And I just wondered if you could help us out with something to kick the doors off the party.'

Tulley's grin broadened. He clearly relished predicting what Ted really wanted. 'I'll be honest with you, Ted.

Nowadays, bar private use, I'm pretty low-key on that front.'

Wait for it.

'Times have changed. Everything's so territorial now. It's not the old days anymore.'

Here it comes.

'But I still keep my ear to the ground, especially for old friends.' He mustered a faux twinkle in his eye.

'You'd be our preferred supplier,' Ted jested.

'I'll see what I can do but if I do go out on a limb for you then your budget'll have to reflect it.'

'Budget isn't an issue.'

Tulley took a sip of his beer, as if celebrating the hardest part of the conversation being over. 'Excellent.'

'We just want some of the entry-level stuff you used to score for Evie.'

'Is Evie afraid to come to me herself now?' He smirked.

Ted considered how to respond. 'She's in a respectable job.'

Tulley snorted. 'Doesn't normally bother her.'

Ted was puzzled. 'Have you seen Evie recently then?'

'Only a couple of weeks ago,' Tulley answered, as if Ted should know. He clocked Ted's expression. 'She not tell you?' He gulped some lager.

'No, think we've had crossed wires.' Ted improvised. 'I thought *I* was sorting out the party entertainment.'

Tulley shrugged. 'That's between you two. Although I don't want an invite if Evie's making the cocktails.'

'What d'you mean by that?'

'Nothing,' Tulley said archly.

'She been hitting you up for Rohypnol?' Ted asked casually.

Tully remained silent but playfully raised an eyebrow.

Ted attempted not to react then shook his head, as if she were incorrigible. 'She's got a seriously warped sense of humour.'

'They both have.'

Ted tried to guess who he could be referring to. How could he extract more details?

'Don't usually get many women buying it. Hope she hasn't been slipping you any.'

'I wouldn't put it past Evie.'

Tulley frowned.

Ted didn't like his expression. 'What is it?'

'Maybe I've said enough.'

Ted wanted to grab Tulley by the scruff of the neck and shake the answer out of him.

'Not lost any time recently? Thought you'd been kidnapped by extra-terrestrials?' Tulley hid his amusement by taking another large swig of lager.

Ted tried to remain calm. 'What are you talking about?'

'Your Mrs, Juliette, she was with Evie when she bought it.'

Chapter 61

Ted attempted to remain focused during his remaining exchanges with Tulley, but he obviously couldn't disguise his reaction to the revelation.

'You OK?' Tulley asked suspiciously.

'Just remembered I've got to be somewhere.' He glanced at his watch and it wasn't a bluff. He was due at his interview with Renton soon.

Tulley didn't seem convinced. 'Sure?'

Ted nodded. 'So, I can contact you via Messenger?'

Tulley slanted his head. 'You tell me exactly what you need, and I'll make some enquiries.'

Ted fought the reflex to stand. 'Cool, I'll send you my wish list.' He extended his hand and Tulley shook it. His grip was tight and palm warm now. 'Was great catching up.'

'We didn't, really.'

Don't walk out too fast.

'Say hi to Juliette and Evie for me.' Tulley showed him his teeth.

'Will do. Be in touch soon.' Ted rose and strolled out as leisurely as he could. Too leisurely? He was meant to be late for an appointment. He picked up his pace and grinned at Tulley's girlfriend. Her face was impassive as she followed him with her eyes.

Had Tulley guessed that he'd just been fishing for who had been buying drugs off him? Ted got into his car and closed the door. What about Kathryn? Did she have anything to do with spiking Jakob? Tulley hadn't mentioned her. He had to speak to Juliette *now*. He took out his phone and dialled. What else was she hiding from him? And how could he possibly conceal this from Renton? He'd ignored his instincts, allowed her to placate him and she'd carried on lying.

Answer service. He called the landline, but nobody picked up. Perhaps she and Zoe were busy with Georgie.

He tried her number again. 'It's Ted. I need to speak to you urgently. Please call back as soon as you get this. We must talk before I see Renton.' He hung up.

But Juliette didn't call him back. When he reached the station, he waited in the car with the phone in his hand, willing her name to appear in the display. Six o'clock. Ted couldn't delay. He got out of the car and ambled to the entrance doors.

He switched the phone off as he went inside. Didn't want to have the conversation he foresaw anywhere near the police station. But what was he going to say to Renton? Would he have to lie for her?

The Dinner Party

'How are you feeling?' Renton gestured to the seat in front of the small desk in the poky interview room.

First question and Ted didn't know how to answer.

His tall male colleague with dyed black hair, Detective Sergeant Patterson, was already seated opposite, iPhone notebook in his hand, attention on the little screen.

'Bewildered.' Ted dropped into the padded chair. He eyed some papers and the interview recorder on the desk.

'Coffee?'

Ted shook his head.

Renton sat and interlinked his stubby fingers. 'I'm so sorry to hear about your friends.'

Ted vaguely nodded. 'I never suspected it of Orla. That she was capable of that.'

'There's been no indicators in the past?'

'No. It was always—' he cut himself off, but then continued. 'If it had been Connor it would have been less of a surprise.'

'Has Mr Connor exhibited suicidal ambition then?'

'In the way he talked recently. I did get concerned enough to mention it to Juliette.'

Patterson started typing on his screen. The sound was turned up and each letter clicked loudly.

Renton didn't seem bothered by it. 'He threatened suicide?'

'Not explicitly. I met him for a drink recently though and he alluded to it. He and Orla have ... had issues.'

'What sort of issues?'

'Passive aggressive stuff. Before they were married even.'

'Anything more than that?'

'Not that I know of. Connor always had a good sense of humour about their bickering, but that changed.'

'You don't know the reason?'

'No.'

'My colleague tells me his condition has stabilized now.'

Why was Renton happy to conduct the interview about what had happened at the railway station without Juliette? But Ted didn't want to ask. Didn't want to precipitate her involvement until he'd had an opportunity to talk to her.

'My colleague said that you'd spoken to Mr Lowney.'

'Very briefly,' Ted confirmed. 'He was on morphine, so he was very drowsy.'

'He didn't say anything to you that you thought significant?'

'Only that Orla apologized to him when she was on the bridge.'

'For what?'

'Something about getting even.'

'Mean anything to you?'

'No. That was it. The nurse told me to leave soon after.'

'I heard he asked only to speak to you.'

'Yes.'

'Don't you think that was odd, that he should demand exactly what Mr Eriksson did when he called you from a payphone after his wife had been murdered and wanted to leave *your* wife out of the conversation?'

268

'I assumed it was because Connor didn't want Juliette to see the state he was in.' But Ted could feel anger at his wife bubbling inside him.

Patterson briefly stopped typing.

Renton leaned back in his chair. 'I've still got Kathryn Driscoll in interview room 8. Thought I'd give her a break. She's been very helpful.'

Ted didn't like the silence that followed the statement. 'She OK?'

'Fine. She told me that the Erikssons and the Lowneys were your wife's friends first.'

'That's right.' And he knew exactly where he was going with it.

The typing started again.

'So it's not strange that they would preclude your wife over you?'

'I know them well too. Jakob became a friend. Perhaps he wanted a male ear, perhaps Connor did too.'

'Or because they wanted to talk to you about something they didn't want your wife to hear.'

'What are you saying?'

'Just thinking out loud. Or it could be something you and the other men want to hide.'

Ted fought to retain his composure. 'It's not.'

'It was your wife that Connor first summoned to the railway station though.'

'Yes.' It was a valid point.

'So that scotches that theory then, doesn't it?'

Ted shrugged. 'Connor wanted my wife there to talk Orla down.' He shivered inwardly again as he recalled her fall from the bridge.

'And Mrs Lowney said nothing to you or your wife before she fell?' Renton examined a piece of paper in front of him.

Ted assumed it was their statement. 'Nothing.'

'No suicide note has been found at the scene or in their house. Why do *you* think she jumped?'

'I really don't know. She looked ... medicated. Like she'd taken a handful of pills.'

'Is that a regular thing?'

'I know she has problems sleeping. I suppose that could have been a contributing factor.'

Renton grimaced, as if he'd tasted the term and it was sour. 'She wasn't anxious about anything?'

'Other than Evie and Jakob's deaths?' Ted said sharply.

'Before that.'

'I hadn't seen Orla for a good few months.'

'You met up with Connor though.'

'Yes, but he didn't mention that Orla was having problems.'

'What about your wife?'

'What about her?' He tried to maintain his patience.

'Was there something on her mind before you all met up this Friday?'

Ted was about to rebuff him but couldn't. Juliette *had* been withdrawn the few weeks leading up to the dinner party.

Chapter 62

'Not that I remember.'

But Renton had picked up on Ted's hesitation. 'Something you want to tell me?'

But Ted wasn't about to pre-empt the conversation he was going to have with Juliette. 'Juliette *is* anxious ...'

Renton opened his eyes wide, prompting him to continue.

'Probably unjustifiably so ...' He had to give Renton something. 'At the dinner party we all played a game ...'

'The trust game?'

'Yes.' Had Kathryn told him during her lengthy interview?

'Mrs Driscoll filled me in on it this afternoon.' Renton seemed to know what he was thinking. 'I'm just wondering why it took so long for any of you to mention it to me.'

Should he say he wanted to all along, that the others had persuaded him not to, that Juliette had been the most vocal about him not talking about it and had gone with Evie to buy the Rohypnol from Tulley? 'It was just a game.' But Ted didn't believe that, had never believed that, even when Evie had first suggested it.

'You didn't think a game about hidden secrets might have had a bearing on what led to Mr Eriksson murdering Mrs Eriksson?'

'It was stupid but ...'

'But?' Renton barked loudly and waited for him to continue.

'Nobody thought that it was responsible for what happened.' He was still lying. For Juliette. What if she was much more involved than he thought and what would happen to their family if she had to be punished for it?

'So why withhold it from me? Because you've all colluded to do so, I have to consider that it's significant.'

'But when Evie and Jakob left, they were drunk but OK.'

'And how were things between you and your wife at the end of the evening?'

'Fine.'

'I've been married. I know what a loaded word "fine" is. You've just played a game of forgiveness. Were you not both wondering what you'd forgiven each other for?'

'Of course.'

'So how were things when you went to bed?'

'We were both exhausted.'

'That isn't an answer.'

Ted inhaled. If it weren't for Juliette, he would have had this conversation the night they'd first met Detective Inspector Renton outside Evie and Jakob's house. 'It was awkward.'

'I should say so. What was discussed?'

'Nothing.'

'Really?'

'There was an atmosphere, but we've talked about it since.'

'You told her what you wrote, and she burnt?'

'Yes.'

That caused Renton to pause. 'And what was that?'

'It was nothing really.'

Detective Patterson looked up from his screen and his sceptical expression matched Renton's.

'I kissed a work colleague of Juliette's. That was all.'

Detective Patterson's clicking began in earnest again.

'And this colleague, a female?'

Ted nodded.

'Would corroborate your story?'

'Yes.'

'If that *is* what you wrote on your piece of paper. We only have your word for that.'

But Ted knew what was coming next.

'And your wife told you her secret, the one you burnt?'

'We didn't ... there wasn't the opportunity. It was in the hospital ...' But he was aware of how lame that sounded.

'And you can't see how the sort of exchanges you two had could have led to similar heated words between Mr and Mrs Eriksson?' Renton was barely controlling his temper. 'A couple who'd had therapy because of their inability to have a family. And between Mr and Mrs Lowney, a couple who already had problems in their marriage?'

273

But it was his fault. He'd chosen to remain silent despite his instincts.

'It filled ten minutes, though, when the dinner conversation had waned after dessert,' Renton said acerbically. 'I have a suspect on CCTV, but now the Erikssons *and* Mrs Lowney are dead. I think the answers lie within your game and more than one of you knows what happened.'

'I've told you everything.'

'I thought you had before.' Renton folded his arms across his broad chest. 'Now I want every detail.'

Chapter 63

Ted went back over what had happened around the dinner table. Twenty minutes later a uniformed officer knocked on the interview room door and Renton ducked out leaving Ted with Detective Sergeant Patterson. His fingers continued clicking on his screen.

Ted acknowledged that he still hadn't heard him speak.

Renton re-entered and appeared flustered. 'Patterson will take the rest of the details.'

His colleague glanced up and frowned.

'A word first.' Renton beckoned the other officer out.

Ted listened to their feet echo off down the corridor and then a door slam. He regarded the unused recorder. He wasn't under arrest. Was he still just helping with inquiries? He took out his phone, switched it back on and checked his screen. No message. Besides needing to speak to Juliette he wanted to make sure she was OK. Was he allowed to make a call? It was unlike her not to return his.

He dialled her, regardless. Answer service. Ted hung up

and strained his ears. No sound from the corridor. He rang the landline at home.

'Hello?'

He immediately recognized the voice. 'Hi, Zoe. Everything there all right? Georgie OK?'

'Yes, he's on his laptop. But Juliette's still not back.'

'What?' Ted tried to calculate how long it had been since he'd left her at Kathryn's house. Had to be over an hour and a half. 'When did you last speak to her?'

'When she called me from the hospital. I was here for Peta to drop Georgie off, but I still haven't heard from her. Will you be back soon? I need to change Pip and all my fresh nappies are next door.'

'I'm sorry. I may be a while longer. I'm at the police station. Have you tried Juliette's number?'

'A few times. I can try again.'

'If you would. And let me know if you have any luck.'

'You sound worried.' Now she did.

'Sure there's an explanation.' But Ted couldn't think of one. 'I'll be there as soon as I can.'

'OK, keep me posted.'

Ted cut the call and clutched the phone. The conversation he needed to have would take a back seat until he knew Juliette was safe. He stood and padded over to the door. What had been so urgent to pull Renton out of their interview?

Should he just walk out? Renton hadn't said he was holding him. He opened the door and looked both ways.

There was room 8. Were they in there with Kathryn? The only activity was the people passing at the far end of the corridor.

His phone buzzed in his hand. Zoe?

Juliette

'Everything OK?' she asked first. But Juliette sounded strange.

Ted returned to the desk and let the door close behind him. 'Yes. I'm still at the station and they haven't let me up for breath.'

'Why are they holding you so long?'

'We can talk later. Why haven't you been picking up?'

'Sorry, just got your message. Had to catch up with Zoe first.'

Ted's next question froze on his lips. She couldn't have spoken to Zoe in the ten seconds he'd just put his head into the corridor. He tried not to let her register the pause. 'Sure you're OK?'

'All under control. Just going to get some dinner for Georgie sorted.'

She wasn't at home. She couldn't be. Juliette hadn't actually said she was, but she'd inferred it.

'Do you want anything?'

'No.' He had to know. 'Can you put Georgie on?'

She hesitated. 'He's in the shower.'

Ted felt his heart slide downwards.

'How much longer will you be?'

Ted scarcely caught the question. 'A while. I'll be home as soon as I can though.'

'OK. We can catch up then.' Her response was upbeat, mimicking the way she always sounded when he phoned to say he would be late.

'I'll ring when I'm on my way.'

'OK, speak then.' Wherever Juliette was, she abruptly hung up.

Ted hurried back to the door and peered into the corridor. As before, the only activity was in the adjoining one. He strode down it and headed quickly for the exit.

Chapter 64

Ted slipped into his car and hastily started it. Would Renton's colleague have got back to the interview room and found it empty yet? He didn't care. He wasn't under arrest and he needed to find Juliette, to speak to her before the police, and he had one idea where she'd be.

Ten minutes later he was pulling into Kathryn and Rhys's road. It was the place he'd left her and that she'd lied about visiting and he was sure her presence there had more significance than the story she and Kathryn had given him.

No sign of Juliette's yellow Fiat 500 on the drive. Ted accelerated by, checking the windows on the way past. There was one light on upstairs. Kathryn was still at the station. Had Rhys returned?

But then he spotted Juliette's empty car parked at the end of the street. He slid in behind it. Ted switched off the engine and went over their recent conversation, trying to pinpoint a reason for him misunderstanding. There was none. He'd told her that he'd been waylaid at the police station; she'd obviously assumed he hadn't phoned Zoe and lied to him.

Ted got out of the car and quietly closed the door. A few lights glowed behind the hedges of the other homes. He made his way along the pavement, the cold air stinging his ears and his face burning hot.

He hung back at the gates to the house and examined the windows again. Just the landing light on. Should he bang the front door or wait for Juliette to leave? Surely she would be heading home soon. Maybe she'd spoken to Zoe by now. If she had she'd know that he'd phoned her. Was she already concocting her next lie to cover whatever she was doing here?

There had to be something going on between Juliette, Kathryn and Rhys. They'd become closer when Juliette's father died. They'd both counselled her through it because they knew what it was like to lose a parent. He recalled coming home from work and finding Kathryn and Rhys in the dining room. Had that experience drawn them even closer together, made them more intimate than he'd realized? It seemed preposterous, but Juliette's car was parked outside and the only light on was upstairs. Ted's stomach shrank as he focused on the pane.

Then Ted remembered how he'd entered the house last time. Kathryn had opened the back door for him. After Rhys had attacked him the three of them had left in a hurry. Had she locked it?

He squinted at the darkened windows downstairs and then kept his eye on the landing as he moved across the driveway and the lawn to the passage at the side, his heartbeat overtaking the quiet echo of his feet.

The Dinner Party

When he got to the end of the path, he took a breath. The smell of rotting compost from the bin there seemed even more overpowering. Ted passed the empty conservatory and took a quick peek in through the double windows beside the back door. It was where he'd found Juliette and Kathryn having their heated conversation that morning, but now the room was unoccupied.

He put his fingers on the cold back door handle and gripped it tight. When he'd stood outside this house the last time he'd told himself that what he found inside might change his perception of Juliette. Now he felt there was no doubt. He tensed, pulled down on the metal and it silently opened.

Ted moved into the dimly lit kitchen, softly closed the door behind him and listened. He could hear the low rumble of the central heating but nothing else. The first aid kit that Juliette had dressed his wound with was on the central breakfast bar next to a bowl of brown bananas. The room smelt vaguely of stale oil. He crossed the pale granite tiles to the doorway to the dingy hall. To his left was the cupboard he'd been locked in to protect him from Rhys.

A muffled thud from above.

Ted clenched his breathing but remained where he was. He waited. Was somebody about to come down the stairs? His body rigidly anticipated Juliette's appearance.

But nobody descended and there was no further noise. Ted followed the ornamental carpet runner to the foot of the stairs and looked to the top. Weak light spilled down them from above. There was no point hesitating. He knew who was up there. Ted put his foot on the bottom stair.

'Please ...'

Ted halted. That was Juliette's voice.

'Please ... don't do this to me,' she implored.

That triggered Ted up the stairs but as he swiftly climbed, he still trod carefully and reached the top without creaking a board. Of the five doors he could see three were sealed, one was open and the other slightly ajar.

'Please ...' Juliette grunted.

Sounded like she was behind the third along that was partially open. Ted stole to it but paused outside. What was he about to walk in on?

'Please ...' she barely whispered.

Ted pushed the door and took in the room. Nobody on or in the double bed. But Ted's relief was fleeting. He could see the back of Juliette's head on the far side of it. She was sitting on the floor.

She'd heard him enter and turned; her expression aghast.

Ted understood why though. He was the very last person she expected or wanted to see. 'Juliette?' Was she hurt? He circled around the end of the bed until he was standing over her.

She looked up at him, but he didn't see her face. He was focused on what she was sitting cross-legged beside. It was long and wrapped in black refuse sacks and a man's hairy right arm protruded from it.

The body was lying at an angle and it appeared that she'd been trying to shift it.

There was a brief moment of pure silence.

Then Juliette was speaking to him. He didn't hear her but bent down, his hands scrabbling for the black plastic over the man's face. His fingers trembled but he easily tore it, the polythene popping and revealing the lifeless features beneath. It was Rhys. His eyes were half closed and there was dried spittle over his beard.

Chapter 65

'Ted ...' she said his name mournfully.

He knew there was to be no explanation, not one that could ever possibly mitigate what he'd found. Ted choked a reaction to Rhys's dead expression and shifted his attention back to her.

She got unsteadily up, and he realized she was barefoot. She was wearing a turquoise silk robe.

'Where are your clothes?' It was his first question.

'In a bag downstairs.' Her gaze was on the floor but not on who lay there.

'Why?' But he'd already guessed. She didn't want to get Rhys's blood on them.

She took a step towards him.

Ted recoiled.

She halted, eyes bulging, as if she had too many things to say that she knew wouldn't make any difference.

'What happened?' Coldness flushed his face.

'It was an accident.'

Nobody needed to dispose of an accident. She was still lying. 'Tell me the truth.'

'I am.'

Ted shook his head.

'Kathryn already asked me to come over this morning. But just before I did Rhys attacked her and she retaliated.'

'Kathryn did this?' Ted looked down at Rhys's twisted position. One arm extended and the fingers curled into his palm.

'Yes.'

He wanted to believe her. 'How?'

'With a glass jug. He'd gone mad and was strangling her on the floor. She managed to get free and hit him as he was getting up. She didn't mean to hit him so hard, but she was terrified. He was out cold. She tied him up so he couldn't attack her again.'

'When?'

'Not long before you arrived this morning.'

'That's crap. Rhys hit me over the head.'

'No, he didn't. Kathryn did.'

Ted was about to rebuke her but realized he hadn't actually seen Rhys before he was slugged. 'When the three of us were in the lounge, I heard a noise upstairs.'

'Yes, Rhys had come round.'

'And when I was locked in the cupboard, he kicked the door.'

'No. That was Kathryn too.'

285

He'd only heard Kathryn shout Rhys's name. 'Why?'

'The police would only have her word that he attacked her. But if you believed he'd attacked you as well ...'

He was stunned by how devious they'd both been. 'And you went along with it?'

'No.' She paused. 'I tried to talk sense into her when you were out cold. I told her we should untie Rhys and call the police. I convinced her. She went upstairs to do it. But Rhys had rolled off the bed and hit his head. That's what you heard when you were talking to us downstairs in the lounge. She couldn't wake him. He'd stopped breathing.'

'Why didn't you tell me what had happened?'

'She said all we had to do was convince you Rhys was still alive when the three of us left the house together. That he'd walked out of here.'

Ted understood but his revulsion swelled further. 'So I was a witness.'

'Kathryn just wanted me to clean everything up while she was at the police station. The plan was to get her and the kids to stay with us for the night straight after she'd been interviewed. Then she'd come back here in the early hours and get rid of him. I was to say I'd got up with Kathryn and kept her company because she couldn't sleep.'

'So she had alibis the whole time. And it would look like Rhys had stormed out and vanished.' Ted was appalled by how calculating they'd been. Had that all been Kathryn?

'But then we got the call from Connor at the railway

station and it all went wrong. Renton kept Kathryn at the police station, so I had to phone her from the hospital.'

'I can't believe you could have been so stupid.'

She turned her back on Rhys, wobbling on her feet. 'We panicked ... but it's done now.'

'What d'you mean, it's done?'

'We've both already lied to the police.'

'*You* haven't yet.'

'I've been cleaning up blood and glass fragments.'

'You were under duress.' But it was going to be impossible to defend what she'd already carried out. 'We have to go to the police right away. It's the only way.'

'You know what will happen if we do,' she said solemnly.

He did, but the alternative was unthinkable. His focus darted to Rhys and away again. How could she even be considering it? How could she have gone this far? 'The police, Juliette. It has to be.'

'What's already happened can't be undone. We could walk out of here, go home. Kathryn will take care of this.'

'Take care of this? Our friend is dead, Juliette.' Anger bled through numbness. 'I won't allow her to do this. And what, we go on telling the lie? How could you live with yourself?'

'Think of Kathryn's girls. Think of Georgie.' There was desperation in her voice.

'Don't. You're not doing that.'

Juliette straightened. 'We walk into the station tonight and I won't be coming back.'

'You didn't kill Rhys. You don't have a criminal record.'

Juliette approached him, reached out.

Again he backed away. He didn't want to be touched by her.

'Think about it. We just walk out of here.'

'He's right, Juliette. Listen to him.'

Ted turned to the doorway.

Kathryn was standing there.

Chapter 66

Ted registered that Juliette wasn't surprised by Kathryn's appearance. 'Where have you come from?'

'The bathroom, cleaning up. Heard you come in through the back.' Kathryn was barefoot and wearing a silk robe too. A canary yellow one.

Ted wondered if they were going to burn both garments once they'd finished. 'I thought you were at the police station.'

'I was. Looked out of my interview room when I heard your voice, saw Renton take you into the other one. I asked an officer if I could go to the canteen. When he OK'd it, I hopped in a cab.'

'To help Juliette?'

'To stop her. She wasn't answering her phone.'

'I didn't want to turn it on when I was here,' Juliette explained.

Made sense. Ted assumed Juliette didn't want any record of her being at the house after that morning. 'So, when you called me earlier ...'

'I drove to the square in town, made the call from there.'

He returned his attention to Kathryn. 'So, why didn't you just confess to Renton?'

'I had to get Juliette out of here first.'

'You've just been trying to talk Juliette out of it?' Ted asked sceptically.

She nodded her bun of hair. It had been tightened to her head again.

'So why are you in a robe as well?'

'She wouldn't listen to me. Made the same argument she just has to you.' Kathryn bit her jaw.

Ted looked at Juliette and she nodded as well. But could he believe anything she said now?

'I won't let the girls grow up without Kathryn,' Juliette said resolutely.

'But if Kathryn confesses now, they may be more lenient,' Ted reasoned.

Juliette shook her head. 'Even if she can leave me out of it, she's tried to cover it up. How will that make her look at a trial?'

Ted held up his hand. 'She's giving you the chance to walk away, Juliette. Take it, for the sake of our family.' He had to seize on Kathryn's approval. 'This was something that happened between *them*.'

Juliette took a deep breath before she answered. 'Because of the game we played around *our* table.'

'Not that again.' Ted felt his blood surge. 'We're not responsible. If anybody's to blame, it's Evie.'

Juliette bit her lip, clearly harnessing her emotions. 'And what about Evie ... and Jakob, and Orla and Connor?'

Ted was silent.

Juliette clenched her fists. 'We can do this. Kathryn's life doesn't need to be ruined as well. Nor the children's. I'm not asking you to do anything except walk out of here.'

'And live a lie. At best. If this goes wrong, I'm an accomplice too. What happens to Georgie then?'

'He's right,' Kathryn reiterated. 'You know he is. This is my situation; I never should have dragged you into it. I panicked. It was selfish.'

Juliette held up her palm. 'Kathryn, we want to do this.'

'No ... we don't,' Ted stated firmly.

'Juliette, listen to him.' Kathryn stood back from the doorway. 'There's no choice. You have to go, both of you. Now.'

Juliette didn't move. 'We're staying.'

'Renton will be looking for me soon.' Kathryn fixed Ted. 'I told him about the game to misdirect him from what we were doing here. But he'll come here to find me. I don't want him to find you two as well.'

'I walked out of the police station too.' Ted glimpsed his watch. 'And I think Renton already knows Kathryn's gone. We can't be seen here. We have to go.'

'Juliette, you're a good friend.' Kathryn's voice was level. 'But you must let me handle this now. You have to leave.'

As the three of them descended the stairs Juliette was

silent. Ted knew there was still a significant conversation to be had but now the only priority was getting out of the house.

'Where are you parked?' Kathryn peered out of the front window.

Ted reached the bottom. 'Near Juliette at the far end of the street.'

'Be a good idea if you both leave the way Juliette came in. Go out the back door and up the lawn. There's an overgrown path at the rear behind the back fence. Follow it round and it should bring you out near your cars at the far end of the road.'

Juliette's expression was pensive.

'Juliette?' Kathryn snapped her out of it. 'You're going out through the kitchen. Quickly. There's a jacket and some of my shoes there. Use those.'

Juliette's face was blank.

'Wait on the decking. I'll keep watch through this front window and give you the word when I'm sure there's nobody in the street to see you get in your cars.'

After Juliette had reluctantly picked up her refuse sack of clothes from the lounge, they walked through the kitchen to the back door.

They both glanced back at Kathryn standing in the hallway and she gestured them through. Juliette slipped on the tan oilskin jacket and green clogs.

'Come on.' Ted opened the back door and they stepped out into the cold air.

The smell of compost hit them as soon as they were

outside. It seemed so much darker than when he'd entered, and their short sharp breaths clouded in front of them.

'We're doing the right thing,' Ted reassured her and closed the door, leaving it open a crack so they could hear Kathryn.

Juliette shivered and checked the frosted pane. 'Please, come with me back inside.'

'We've done that discussion. We have to go.'

Her eyes met his. 'Please ...'

Ted squinted to the fence at the far end of the lawn. Only trees lay beyond it. He saw the gate to the rear path there. They could leave undetected and he assumed it led to the end of the short road. 'We'll talk at home.'

'Let's go back in.'

He felt his stomach quaking against the cold and what he'd just seen upstairs. 'There are still questions you need to answer.'

'Please, Ted. I really think we should go back inside.'

Ted ignored her plea. 'Like why the hell you would be buying Rohypnol from Grant Tulley.'

Juliette's features froze and then her gaze slid sideways.

Ted turned and realized that there was a figure stood behind the frosted pane of the back door. Wasn't Kathryn meant to be shouting from her position at the front window? The door was swiftly tugged open.

'No!' Juliette yelled.

Ted held up a hand to block his attacker, but all he could do was watch as the kitchen knife jabbed down hard, straight into the middle of his chest.

Chapter 67

Ted emitted a gasp and looked down at the handle jutting from his chest and then up at Kathryn. Her revulsion for what she'd done was quickly replaced by panic. The blade was stuck in his sternum, the metal lodged in bone. He went to grab the weapon, but she lunged forward and pulled it out to stab him again.

Ted rammed his way back into the kitchen, using his body weight to repel her and protect Juliette. But Kathryn already had a proper grip on the knife, and he felt the blade thrust into his stomach. He heard himself grunt but kept moving forward.

Kathryn's bare feet slipped on the tiles and she slammed hard on her back, the knife sliding deeper into Ted as he landed on top of her. The air was squeezed out of her lungs and sour breath was in his face.

Kathryn's eyes were wide open, and she gagged for air as his body pressed down on hers. But Ted remained motionless. He didn't want to move or let the blade go any deeper.

He reached down between them and firmly grasped the handle with his right hand.

He closed his eyes as he felt the warmth there. Juliette was screaming at Kathryn, but he focused on remaining still.

Kathryn released the handle and he felt her trying to wriggle out from under him. Ted fought to keep her pinned there but her nails were digging into his face. She growled and applied more pressure. He felt the points pierce his cheeks, but Ted just prayed she wouldn't do the same to his eyes and used his free left hand to hold the blade even tighter.

Kathryn slipped away and he took his weight on his knees and looked up to see Juliette harshly grabbing the bun of Kathryn's hair before she could get to her feet.

'Get off him!' Juliette used both hands to wrench Kathryn's head back.

But Kathryn punched up at her and caught her hard under the jaw.

Briefly stunned, Juliette let go of her hair with one hand and Kathryn seized her opportunity and stood upright, twisting her head and slugging Juliette full in the face. Juliette staggered back and Kathryn immediately went for the knife block on the breakfast bar.

If she got hold of another blade, Juliette was dead. Ted reached out with one hand and snagged her ankle. He dragged her away from the block.

Swivelling on the other foot she leaned against the bar and kicked at his face. Ted tucked his cheek against his shoulder as she stamped at his skull with her heel. It felt like a sledgehammer and his teeth squeaked as he gritted them against the assault.

After the fourth or fifth blow Ted heard a fizzing noise in his ear and knew he wasn't going to be able to take much more. He didn't want to move from his spot though and disturb the steel that was in his gut.

The pummelling ceased and Ted looked up to see Kathryn reaching around for one of the knives in the block. Juliette had fallen against the oven and there was blood streaming from her nose.

Ted yanked hard on Kathryn's foot and she fell onto her back and groaned with the impact. She immediately rolled and started getting up again.

Ted had to move fast to intercept her. He rose and stumbled with her to the bar. Reached out and grabbed a knife handle. As her fingers extended to the block he pushed the whole thing forward.

The block slid across the bar and clattered over the other side, the handle remaining in his hand revealing the weapon he was holding. It was the thick blunt steel for sharpening knives.

Ted felt the knife judder in his stomach as Kathryn jerked back against him, trying to break free. He couldn't allow her to get to the other side of the bar. Her uncoiled hair was in his face, her spine pressing the blade as he tried to hold it in place with his other hand.

'Kathryn ...' Juliette was groggily trying to get up again.

'Let me go!' Kathryn was about to break free.

There was nothing else for it. Ted swung the sharpening steel against the back of her head. Once. She was still fighting him. Twice and harder, she stopped. On the third strike she crumpled.

He lurched back and let her body drop hard to the tiles. For the first time, Ted looked down at the knife handle lodged in his stomach. A huge patch of dark red saturated his blue shirt; his fingers were completely coated as well. As the room canted, Ted felt his legs tremble and give way.

'Ted!' Juliette caught him as he collapsed sideways and lowered him to the floor.

Chapter 68

'I've called an ambulance. Ted!'

Ted opened his eyes to see Juliette crouching on her knees beside him, still wearing the tan oilskin jacket. He was lying on his side.

'Don't move.'

A large pool of blood had crept away from him across the granite tiles to where Kathryn lay motionless. He could see dark red in the roots of her hair. Had he killed her?

'I don't want to pull the knife out. Hold on. They'll be here soon.'

He felt freezing and could vaguely feel Juliette's hot fingers gripping the top of his arm. 'You knew ... you knew she was going to attack me.' He only hissed.

'Don't speak. Stay still.'

'You're going to have to tell me what—' he tugged in a painful breath.

'Please, don't speak.'

'You talk then. I don't know if the ambulance is going to be here in time.' Ted watched as his blood inched forward again.

'Ssshhh. You'll be fine,' Juliette's voice trembled.

'Tell me,' he said sharply and felt his fingers slip around the handle. 'Grant Tulley ...'

Juliette said nothing but squeezed his arm. 'It was for Orla,' she eventually whispered.

Ted shook his head.

'Connor was working late all the time and she was sure he was sleeping with other women. She went out one night, met another man. He drugged and raped her. She didn't tell Connor.'

Ted looked up and she was staring at Kathryn.

Juliette wiped caked blood from her nostrils with the back of her hand. 'Kathryn told me about it, about what she and Evie were going to do to get even for Orla. I wanted to be part of it. I went with Evie to get the Rohypnol from Grant Tulley first. The next night Evie went into the same nightclub where Orla had met the guy who raped her. Orla, Kathryn and I waited in the delivery yard at the back. Evie got talking to him and sent us a photo of him with her phone. Orla confirmed it was him. His name was Steve North. He was a sleazeball.'

That name sounded familiar to Ted.

'Evie slipped the Rohypnol into his drink. Then she led him out to the yard. He was out of it and Orla beat him black and blue. Took it too far. He was lying on the floor while she stamped on him, all over his face. He stopped moving.' She swallowed. 'We left him there. Next morning the local news said his body had been found.'

Ted recalled it. The guy – a petty thief and a dealer – had died of head injuries behind McCoy's nightclub. The police suspected a gang. It was the story that had given Georgie nightmares. When was that, a couple of weeks ago? That coincided with the distinct change in Juliette's mood.

'Orla withdrew, like she hadn't even been part of it. She hadn't begun to absorb what she'd done. What we'd all done. Evie suggested the game.'

Ted thought of them sitting in the hospital waiting room earlier that day and Juliette assuring him that they could survive the secret that he'd needed to confess. 'You knew, before the evening began?'

Juliette didn't respond but a tear rolled down her cheek.

'And Georgie overheard you in the kitchen planning it with Evie beforehand.' Ted couldn't feel the handle of the knife anymore. 'So Jakob *hadn't* attempted suicide before.'

'No. Evie was going to crack because Jakob knew there was something wrong. She wanted to play the game to absolve herself, all three of us did. That's why we didn't want Renton to know about us playing it: one of us was bound to slip up. When I spoke to Evie early that morning, after the dinner party, she said she'd put all the Rohypnol she had left in a drink for Jakob when they got home. She'd drunkenly told him part of what had happened at McCoy's but then panicked. He was already pretty out of it and she wanted him to forget their conversation because of what it would mean for the rest of us. But he had a bad reaction to the Rohypnol and started getting violent.'

'Who went to their house before us?' But Ted already suspected.

'Kathryn. Evie called her first, so she slipped out while Rhys was still sleeping. When she arrived, Evie had left the door on the catch for her. Jakob had chased Evie onto the back lawn and was strangling her. Kathryn hit him with a garden ornament, but it was too late. Before she left, she tried to find Jakob's drink with the drug in it. She looked all over the house for it, but Evie must have poured it away. That's why she was upstairs when we arrived.'

Ted remembered the person coming down the stairs and slipping out through the front after they'd entered the house.

'But she needed Rhys to lie to the police when they were asked about the phone call that Evie made to them.'

'So, that story about her having an affair with Rhys's brother ...' he croaked.

'A lie. I was meant to be seeing her on Monday morning. She was worried about her interview with Renton. But she confessed to Rhys about what happened at Evie and Jakob's. He was beside himself, wanted her to go to the police, but she couldn't face the notion of a prison sentence and leaving her girls. It turned into a fight. That's when she hit him with the jug.'

The room dimmed and Ted considered the intricate story Juliette had told him about Kathryn's affair and what had happened after Rhys had supposedly struck him. 'And Kathryn wanted you to cover things up.'

'The rest is true. She wanted to convince you that Rhys was still alive while she got rid of him. I shouldn't have convinced her to carry on when she got here tonight. I knew exactly what she meant just now when we were upstairs and she said she'd handle things.'

Ted wondered at what point Kathryn had decided she had to kill him. When he'd just been outside the back door and said he knew about them buying the Rohypnol from Grant Tulley, had that made her mind up? 'But if she had killed me, then what?'

'She talked to me about setting the house on fire with Rhys inside.'

'And maybe me as well.' Ted felt his head getting heavy.

'She was only thinking about the girls and how she couldn't let them go. That's why I wanted you to agree to helping her: so that she wouldn't harm you.'

Ted's blood trickled further towards Kathryn. His eyelids drooped and it felt like he was melting into the floor. Where was the ambulance?

Her hand gripped his arm tighter. 'Just hold on.'

Chapter 69

Something yanked Ted back. Was Juliette speaking to him again, trying to keep him conscious?

But as he focused, Ted could see the soles of Juliette's bare feet. They'd lost Kathryn's green clogs and were red with blood. She was lying face up and Kathryn was sitting astride her chest with her back to him, her shoulders tensed and head quaking. She was strangling Juliette.

A smothered exclamation, a long strain of exertion.

Ted couldn't tell if it was Juliette's or Kathryn's. Ted stirred his muscles but felt the pain of the blade like he was being stabbed again. He groaned and the energy immediately drained from his limbs. He could scarcely move.

Ted could see his blood had been smudged around the tiles by Juliette's thrashing legs. His mouth opened to scream at Kathryn, but he stopped himself. She must think he was still out cold.

Kathryn's shoulders locked and the exclamation halted. She was squeezing the last breath out of Juliette. Ted managed to slide himself forward, but his body felt as if it were starting to dissolve. Covering the distance seemed suddenly impossible.

Juliette's legs were slowing as the life left her limbs and Kathryn maintained the pressure.

Ted put his one hand beside him, and his fingers slipped in his cold blood.

Juliette stopped kicking but kept twitching. Kathryn remained rigid as she waited for her to be completely motionless.

Leaning on one hand Ted curled up his legs and then pushed himself forward, his bulk sluggishly slithering along the wet tiles so that he was almost upon them. But he was still over two feet away.

Kathryn turned to see him crouching there. There was no alarm on her face. She kept her stolid eyes fixed on him while she waited for Juliette to die.

Ted's perspective shuttered and went black. He had to stay awake. Gripping the knife handle hard the agony brought him round. He pulled the blade from his stomach, felt the metal draw across his innards and a gush of warm liquid as the point came out. He heard himself gasp.

But Kathryn just watched him, calculating whether he was really a threat or if he was about to pass out again. 'I had to do this, Ted.' A tear glistened in her left eye. Juliette had stopped moving. 'Like Evie, that night on the back lawn. She wanted to go to the police. I'd already slugged

Jakob. Thought he was dead. The ornament was still in my hand. I had to stop her too.'

She'd murdered Evie. Ted felt as if everything was slowing down. He was on the verge of sliding back into unconsciousness. Was Kathryn going to set fire to the house as Juliette had said? What new lies would she use to justify what she'd done? But the peril Juliette was in and his reaction to it seemed to be receding.

Had to help her.

A weight was pressing him to the floor; the burden of staying awake was too much.

Kathryn clenched her jaw. Lifted herself to completely crush Juliette's throat.

He gathered all his strength and lunged, struck Kathryn hard in the back.

They were on the floor, all three of them. Where was the knife? It was no longer in his grip. He clasped Kathryn's leg.

Kathryn was reaching up, yanking on the drawer.

Its loud crash to the floor was like a depth charge, the room and its vivid detail brightly flooding Ted's vision.

There was cutlery and utensils scattered around them. Hands including his were scrabbling for a weapon.

Kathryn seized something.

Ted registered it was a long metal prong with a small black box with a digital screen attached. It was a stainless-steel skewer for testing the temperature of meat.

As Kathryn turned and brandished it, he held up his palm for protection and felt the sharp end pierce it. He scarcely registered the injury, just needed to disarm her as blackness crowded everything out. He kept hold of her leg but could feel his fingers weakening.

Ted felt the prong jab hard in his back and his whole frame stiffened against the acute sensation of the new wound. He tried to rise but couldn't. How deeply had it been planted in him? Was he paralyzed? He could still move his arms.

'Let go!' she spat.

He wasn't about to. He clung hard to her leg, dug his nails into her warm calf and skated forward on his front through the smeared blood on the granite tiles. If he relinquished it he knew the outcome that already felt so imminent would arrive even sooner.

Their three bodies thrashed around on the tacky floor and noisily scattered utensils.

A scream.

It tugged him back. He'd passed out again. Consciousness was as slippery as his grasp on the leg, which jerked from under him before a bare foot caught him full in the face. The harsh impact deadened his hearing, warm blood filled his left nostril and darkness closed on his thoughts like a snare.

Wake up!

But his internal voice was being suffocated and scarcely penetrated the barrier his brain was erecting against the assault.

Wake up.

No urgency in the muffled command now. He was

withdrawing, leaving physical sensations far behind. Oblivion beckoned.

'Ted!'

His eyelids shot open. The return to the kitchen was as painful as his injuries.

His hand was empty. She'd got free. The consequences of that rushed into him as fast as the room.

'Ted!' It was Juliette.

He saw Kathryn's face, shock suspending her expression.

Juliette. She was standing. The bloodied knife he'd taken from his stomach was in her hand, and she'd thrust the blade half inside Kathryn's neck.

Kathryn's hand went to the injury and blood poured over her fingers and the canary yellow collar of her robe. She turned to Juliette, uncoiled hair bisecting her expression, lips open as the red torrent cascaded from the wound.

Black flooded in. Ted was swept away.

Chapter 70

'Georgie!' Raising his voice resonated the wound in his stomach and activated the jagged pain in his back. But the doctors had said it had only been a matter of luck the knife hadn't severed any main arteries or pierced Ted's liver and that the prong had just missed his spine.

'Coming now!' Georgie usually had to be summoned a couple of times, but over the three months of Ted's recovery he'd been quick to respond.

Ted heard Georgie scuttle along the landing and waited for him as he descended the stairs. 'I have to go now. Zoe's here.'

Georgie reached the bottom of the stairs and nodded despondently.

Georgie used to get excited about Zoe sitting him, but she was now a daily visitor. Every weekday Peta picked him up from school and handed him over to Zoe until Ted came home. The time that had followed his struggle in the kitchen with Kathryn had been a blur of hospital appointments, visits to Juliette and interviews with Detective Inspector Renton.

'I've left money for lunchtime pizza. Zoe's got the menus. Save me some stuffed crust.' He tried to make it sound like fun.

'When will she be coming home?'

'I'm hoping to find that out today.' Ted had noticed Georgie had started calling Juliette 'she'. He'd said that if the police were holding his mother then she must have done something wrong, like Auntie Kathryn. Ted had tried to explain but, without giving him the specifics, it was difficult to convince him otherwise.

Zoe had told Ted that the story had broken on TV soon after he'd been taken to hospital, so the kids at Georgie's school were bound to be telling him things he'd rather have contained. Georgie had stopped asking questions about his Auntie Evie, Uncle Jakob, Uncle Rhys, Auntie Orla, and Auntie Kathryn but Ted was sure they occupied his thoughts as much as his.

'Brendan said they're going to throw away the key.'

Ted tried not to react. He sat down on the third stair up from the bottom and patted the space beside him.

Georgie seated himself.

'You don't say "she", OK?'

Georgie nodded reluctantly.

'We all help our friends. You'll understand. But some-times you have to draw the line, particularly if you're breaking the law.'

'Like when you visited Uncle Jakob in the park?'

'Yes. That was a very difficult decision to make.'

'Even though you couldn't help him.'

Every morning he woke with the image of him hanging lifelessly from a tree, a desperate act of suicide for a crime he hadn't committed. Evie, Jakob, Rhys, Orla and Kathryn; would they all have shared the same fate if they hadn't played the trust game? However it happened, Ted figured that, sooner or later, the truth of what the four women had done to Steve North would have surfaced.

Juliette was being sentenced at one, and Ted had taken Georgie out of school for the day. He knew his classmates were mercilessly teasing him, even though Ted had asked his head teacher to step in. 'Remember what I said about ulterior motives? Just don't let your friends lead you down the wrong path.' He tried not to imagine Juliette, Kathryn and Evie watching while Orla assaulted Steve North.

'Shouldn't you try to save your friends from doing it though?'

He nodded. 'Just surround yourself with people you can trust.' Connor had visited him at home the previous Wednesday. He was bringing up two children alone now, and Ted was determined to help him deal with what had happened. He still didn't know what his secret was or Jakob and Rhys's but compared to what the game had been orchestrated for they were probably as insignificant as his. 'Maybe your current friends don't appreciate you're a good guy, but the next ones might.'

'But I don't think I'll meet any new friends.'

Ted was going to tell him he would, that it would happen. But right then both of them were in the same boat.

The night around the table still played back in his head – the girls' reactions and glances and the expression on Juliette's face when he burnt her envelope with her secret inside. Had she really thought that was an end to it? Or maybe the four women knew that was a sure way to begin to expose what they'd done. None of them could have foreseen how badly it could have gone wrong. He shook the image of Juliette planting the knife in Kathryn's neck and looked at his watch. 'I'm late. Got to go.' He stood and so did Georgie.

Georgie took a lavender envelope out of his pocket and handed it to him. 'It's a good luck card for her. I made it today.'

Ted examined it. Georgie had unwittingly used one of the remaining envelopes that Juliette had at the dinner party. Her secret had been inside a lavender one. 'That was a nice thing to do.' He would dispose of the envelope before he gave it to Juliette. 'I'll be back in a few hours.' He shouted down the hall. 'Zoe, I've got to go!'

She came up the hallway nursing Pippa. 'Hope it all goes well.'

Ted acknowledged that she was wearing bright lipstick again. She always did when she came round now. A fact he was studiously ignoring.

'Come on you.' She rallied Georgie. 'Let's order those pizzas.'

Georgie plodded down the hallway towards her. 'We have to get stuffed crust for Dad.'

'We won't forget Dad.' She smiled at Ted.

'And what are we going to do after that?' Georgie asked her.

She stepped to one side so he could pass and touched his head as he did. 'Who knows? Let's see what happens when he gets back.' She kept smiling, held Ted's gaze for a few seconds longer than was comfortable and then escorted Georgie to the dining room.

Ted watched them go but lingered in the hallway and listened.

'Alexa, play Zoe's playlist,' the babysitter instructed.

Some synth pop kicked off and Ted could no longer hear what she was saying to his son.

Acknowledgements

First of all, big thanks to you, the reader, for selecting this story and allowing my dinner party characters to live in your head. I hope they were worthwhile guests. Without your imagination books are redundant.

I couldn't write without my faithful support base, namely my patiently wonderful and wonderfully patient wife, Anne-Marie, and my Mum and Dad, who are all experts when it comes to creating a loving atmosphere around a dining table.

At big debt of gratitude goes to Finn Cotton, my astute editor at HarperCollins, who enthusiastically seized on this idea and ran with it. I appreciate the insightful notes along the way and those too of Janette Currie, my copy editor.

A very special thank you to author, Noelle Holten, who has consistently championed my work and was instrumental in getting this picked up. Hope you still have time to read my stories as well as creating your own!

And, as ever, I can't underestimate how grateful I am for the time spent by reviewers and bloggers who are such a vital cog in every author's career. Thanks for your generosity online but, moreover, for giving up your valuable time so other readers can enjoy the wealth of great writing out there. A special salute to Karen Cole, Jen Lucas, Nicki Richards, Donna Maguire, Zoe-lee O'farrell, Nigel Adams, Suze-Clarke-Morris, Kaisha Jayneh, Berit and Vicci at Audio Killed The Bookmark, Katie Jones at The Book Cave, Amanda Oughton, Emma C. at Booking Good Read, Sean Talbot, Rachel Broughton, Alison Drew, Magdalena Johansson, Diane Hogg, Renita D'Silva, Martha Cheeves, Joyce Juzwik, Amy Sullivan, Kelly Lacey, Norma Farrelly, Rebecca Pugh, Claire Knight, Chelsea Humphrey, Ellie Smith, Lorraine Rugman, Steve Robb, Emma Welton, Stephanie Rothwell, Cleo Bannister, Abby Fairbrother, Sarah Hardy, Meggy Roussel, Sheila Howes, Linda Strong, Maxine Groves, Joanne Robertson, Susan Hampson, Kate Moloney, Eva Merckx, Jules Mortimer, Mandy White, Malina Skrobosinski, James Atkins, Kaz Lewis, Fran Hagan, Stephen Edger, James Garcia Jr, Shell Baker, Mandie Griffiths, Jo Ford, Marilina Tzelepi and Scott Griffin.

Please swing by my website for all the latest: richard@richardjayparker.com or find me on Instagram (bemykiller), Twitter (@Bookwalter) and Facebook (RichardJayParkerFans).